AWAKENED MAGIC

THE WOLF BORN TRILOGY

JEN L. GREY

Cover Designed by Orina Kafe

CHAPTER ONE

My heart pounded as Brock's teeth sank into my neck. I tried desperately to push him away, but the two shifters had my arms and legs pinned to the giant bed. The more I jerked, the harder their hands gripped me, cutting off my circulation.

Out of every possibility, I hadn't imagined this. My entire world had come to a halt. I cried out in pain and terror, trying to move my head to try to smash his face in between my head and shoulder so he had to retract his teeth before it was too late.

Then, his emotions poured into me: terror, anxiety, and anger—nothing that made sense.

One thing was clear, though: he'd claimed me against my will. I felt violated and insignificant, the exact emotions he'd hoped to get from me.

"Why?" My voice broke, and his feelings of power flowed through the bond.

He stood, a cocky smirk in place, and wiped the blood from his mouth. His silver eyes darkened to gray, and in this god-awful, bright white room, the auburn highlights in his usual chestnut brown hair were vivid. "Because you needed to know there is no way you're getting out of this."

Like hell there wasn't. I refused to be forced into a mate bond I didn't want. I'd never claim him as mine and sleep with him to set the bond into action. Only one person was meant for me.

Donovan.

My heart fractured at his name.

The two shifters released their hold on me, and my hand went straight to my neck. My fingertips touched the pronounced indentions and slipped across the warm blood trickling down my neck. Between that and the metallic scent, my stomach recoiled, and bile inched up my throat.

Acting like the typical alpha heir, Brock motioned to the two shifters. "Let's give her time to get herself together."

"Wait," Tommy said as he moved his head to the side so his shaggy, mousy brown hair moved out of his boring brown eyes. He was skinny. I could've taken him, but with two wolf shifters holding me down, I didn't have a chance. "Don't you want to make her bite you back?"

I already hated the shifter for alerting Brock that I'd been back at Kortright University. My pack, Egan, and the vampires had faced near-constant attacks because I was a hybrid—fae and wolf. The fae were elitist and saw anything that wasn't pure-blooded fae as a threat that had to be eliminated. We'd returned to Kortright because I'd run into a fae there right before we'd vanished. I'd needed her to hide my fae's magic, not realizing that the man I'd grown up believing was my dad and the alpha heir he'd promised me to had sent people to watch the school.

I should've known better.

The wolves had descended, quite literally, and we'd been outnumbered. I'd gotten captured while trying to get revenge for my fated mate. Four wolves had attacked him and injured him. Egan, the dragon shifter, had taken care of three of them, but one had gotten away, and I'd chased him right to Brock. If I'd been thinking clearly, things would have been different, but maybe it had worked out for the best. If Brock had found me, he'd have known that both Donovan and Axel were alive. Donovan and Axel probably would've been captured too and brought here to die. At least, I didn't have to worry about that.

"No, the mating ceremony is Friday." Brock snickered, enjoying my terror. "I can wait until then." He closed the distance between us and rubbed his thumb across my cheek. "Though it might be hard."

His touch didn't completely repulse me like it had every other time, which terrified me. That couldn't happen. My heart belonged to another.

"I'll see you soon, baby," he cooed and walked to the door. As he exited with the other two shifters, Brock commanded, "Stand guard outside. She doesn't go anywhere alone."

I was their prisoner, but I had to focus on holding myself together. If that took me channeling all of my rage toward them, then so be it.

The door shut, leaving me alone in the horrible room. I stumbled to the oval mirror and looked at myself. My ocean-blue eyes seemed sunken, and my rose-gold hair lay limp on my shoulders. I needed a shower after having a bag over my head the entire way here from the school, which had to be at least a couple of hours.

Even though I didn't want to, I opened my pack bond to Roxy, Axel, and Donovan. I had to get out of here before they forced me to claim Brock and completely ruined my bond with Donovan.

Sadie? Donovan's deep, husky voice brought tears to my eyes. *Stop shutting down the bond.*

His anger and concern stripped me bare. *I'm sorry.* I needed to hold it together, but how could I? Another man had claimed me. It shouldn't have happened. Everything was wrong. A sob racked my body.

What's wrong? Donovan asked, his emotions raw.

If I could feel him this clearly, they had to know how upset I was. *I ...* I had to tell him. He'd find out sooner or later.

Girl. Roxy's sassy attitude linked with me. *Tell me or I'll kick your ass.*

When she said ridiculous things like that, it usually made me smile, but not this time. I normally would have retorted something like, "How? You aren't even here." Or something equally cheesy, but I didn't have it in me to pretend. *Brock. He ...* Damn, this was so hard.

Donovan's low growl filled my head. *He what, Sadie?*

He ... I inhaled sharply. *Bit me.*

What? Roxy almost yelled. *He bit you? Like on your neck?*

I'm thinking that's a yes since she's struggling to get it out. Axel sounded strange. I'd never heard him talk like that before.

He had two people hold me down. I couldn't say more. They could use their imagination for the rest. *I need to get out.*

Is that all he did? Donovan asked so low it could have passed as a whisper.

Yes. At least, he hadn't pushed for more. *That was it.*

Did you bite him back? His voice cracked.

No, I would never. He had to know that. *But they're arranging a mating ceremony for Friday. I have to get out of here before then.* To solidify the claim, I'd have to bite him back and then have sex. As long as I got out of here before that, my bond with Donovan wouldn't be erased. It couldn't come to that.

Donovan's anger slammed into me through our bond. *Two days? Like hell I'm going to allow that to happen.*

Damn straight. Roxy's determination rang clear. *Now, where the hell are you? We're tracking your ass to Atlanta. Do you know how big of a fucking city that is?*

That makes sense. Even though they live in Chattanooga, their business is down here. They want me to be hard to find. I'm looking out the window for any clue as to where I am, but all I see are brick buildings across the road.

Just calm down, Donovan said soothingly. *We're on our way to you. It's slow going, but we're following the bond.*

I should be able to see an intersection from the other side of the house. I scanned the room, hoping to find something with the building name or anything with a landmark.

The clock beside the white king-sized bed said it was after ten at night, and I was exhausted. I couldn't do anything right now, and if I tried to leave, those two assholes would follow me. I didn't want to be anywhere near them after what had happened. *I'll look for clues tomorrow morning. If I go out and look around, Tyler and the shifters will get suspicious.*

Ugh ... of course, that prick is there too. Roxy sounded as disgusted as I felt. *Get some rest and wake up early. Maybe you can snoop around before anyone gets up.*

That sounded like a good plan. *Yeah, that's what I'll do.*

I got up early pretty often, so it wouldn't be too suspicious. I set the alarm on the clock by the bed and turned down the volume so only I would hear. Those two idiots at my door should be gone by then.

Mom flashed into my mind. *Are Mom and Titan okay?* They'd been waiting for us at the cars on the other side of the woods. They hadn't been around when it had all gone down.

Yeah, they're fine, Roxy reassured me. *They're here with us. Winter refused to be left behind.*

I'd have refused too, but knowing they were okay made a world of difference. *All of you need to be careful.*

I hate this, Donovan said, sounding defeated. *But you've had a shit day. You need some rest. Are you sure you're safe?*

No, I wasn't, but I didn't want to worry him anymore. *Yeah, I'm going to lock the door and put a chair under the doorknob.* It wouldn't prevent someone from entering, but it would alert me. I walked over to the all-white vanity, grabbed the white chair, and carried it to the door. *I'll figure out something more definitive in the morning.* I wasn't sure how long I could stand being here.

Okay. He wasn't thrilled, but we had no other option. *Let me know if anything goes wrong.*

I checked my emotions, holding them tight. *I will.* It was a lie, but they didn't know that. They couldn't smell the sulfur smell from my fib via the link.

And girl. Roxy linked back with me. *Find a weapon. If that asshole tries something again or forces you to bite him, cut off his balls.*

How I wished I'd had something earlier. Between Tyler informing me that he knew I wasn't his daughter and Brock forcing half a claim on me, I wasn't sure I could take anything else tonight. *On it.*

I didn't close the connection fully but locked it down. I wasn't in the mood to chat, and I needed to feel my emotions without each and every one of them knowing how broken I felt. I glanced around the white walls, and my eyes settled on a door near the bed.

Curiosity moved my feet, and I opened the door and turned on the lights. The door led to a large walk-in closet filled with clothes.

I grabbed a few outfits, and my heart sank. They were all my size. Tyler must have sent people out to buy clothes for me. I spun around to find stylish shoes in my size. Holy shit. How long had they planned on bringing me here? Probably since the day I'd run away. They hadn't even considered that they might not find me.

Not wanting to see any more, I stumbled out of the closet and toward the bathroom. I needed a hot shower to loosen up my muscles. I'd ridden in the car with my hands cuffed behind my back for so long that my back and shoulders screamed in discomfort.

When I entered the bathroom, I wasn't surprised. The entire room matched the bedroom. All-white tile, a white sink, a large white tub, and a white marble walk-in shower. Whoever had designed this room must have thought this was chic, but in reality, it was overkill.

A linen closet sat at the other end of the room. I shut and locked the door, needing to feel some sort of comfort. After turning on the water, I snatched a towel and slowly removed my clothing. I stepped into the water, relishing the warmth, and turned so it hit my back.

The whole day came crashing down on me.

I placed my head under the showerhead and let the water mix with my tears. I'd never felt so broken before. In a day, not only had I found out I'd been lied to my entire life, but all my choices had been stripped away from me. I hated feeling vulnerable and afraid. I thought I'd put that part of my life aside, but here I was, feeling weaker than ever.

I'd recently found my mother and grandparents, only to have them ripped away again. Donovan and I had almost completed our mate bond, but the fae had interrupted it. Now Brock had stolen that from me. He'd claimed me, preventing Donovan from being able to do it. Right when I'd thought I'd found my place and a chance at happiness, Tyler had stolen it all.

What had I ever done to deserve this? Not only had I grown up without a mother because I'd thought she was dead, but I found out I'd never have a chance to meet my real father. Tyler had killed him, taking yet another thing from me.

The hurt suffocated me until I couldn't breathe. *Dammit, Sadie. Get yourself together. We can't fall apart ... not now.*

To survive this, I had to get it together. I quickly washed my hair and body with the same soaps I used back at my childhood home. Another little thing courtesy of Tyler, I was sure.

As I stepped out of the shower, I toweled off and slipped my clothes back on. I refused to use the clothes they'd bought for me. I'd rather stink and wear these clothes as an act of defiance.

Not bothering to brush my hair, I trudged back into the room and flopped on top of the huge-ass bed. Even with the lights off, the white hurt my eyes. I climbed under the covers, using them as protection, and curled up against a large, stiff pillow.

My breathing grew steady, but I tossed and turned, unable to sleep. I missed Donovan's arms around me. He and I had slept together every night since we'd run from Kortright to hide with Lillith and Katherine's vampire nest.

Needing to hear his voice, I opened my link to just him. *Hey. You there?*

His response was immediate. *Of course I am. Is everything okay?*

No. I missed him so damn much. *I wish you were here.*

I'd do anything to take your place. He sounded miserable. *We're on foot, heading to you.*

On foot? It'd be faster in a car. *Why?*

We can't follow the tug in the car. He sighed in frustration. *We kept driving in circles. We're going to find you and get Katherine and Lillith to meet us there.*

Is everyone okay? Donovan had gotten hurt, not too long ago. *Don't you need to rest and heal?*

I'm better, he said shortly. *I won't rest until I find you.*

I love you. He had to know that, no matter what happened. *And I swear, I won't claim him and complete the bond. I'd rather die than lose you forever.*

I love you too, and it won't come to that. I will find you before the ceremony. He projected his feelings toward me. *Now get some rest, and let me know when you're awake.*

There wasn't anything left to say. *Okay. Good night.*

The connection ended, and I lay there blinking, still unable to fall asleep.

THE ALARM BUZZED, waking me from what little sleep I'd managed. I blinked as reality crashed back over me.

Shit. I had to get up and snoop while I could.

I jumped out of bed and tiptoed to the door like someone might overhear. I was being ridiculous, but it gave me some semblance of control.

I clutched the chair leaning against the doorknob and

moved it slowly, not making a sound. I stilled and listened, making sure no one walked by.

The musky smell of shifter was missing, so dumb and dumber were gone. I unlocked the door and opened it slowly. I stuck my head out the door and glanced both ways down the hallway.

Empty.

Good. I'd hoped it would be this way. I stepped into the hallway and retraced my steps from the night before. After taking two steps, a door opened behind me, and the overwhelming smell of shifter hit my nose.

CHAPTER TWO

"What are you doing?" Brock asked sleepily.

Just my luck that it would be him. But Tyler seemed like a worse alternative. I grimaced at the thought.

When had I started equating Brock as being a step above Tyler? I didn't want to know that answer.

Forcing my heart to remain calm, I turned to face him. After all, I could at least explain it away with the truth. "I want to get familiar with the ... house?" I wasn't sure if it was a house.

"It's a condo." He yawned, but the weariness in his eyes was evident. "I own the first three floors. The bottom floor is an entryway to the elevator for those without garage access. They screen everyone thoroughly."

His pompous attitude might come in handy. If I could get him talking, I could maybe learn where we were.

"Go back to sleep," I said. I didn't want to spend any more time than necessary with him. My stomach grumbled, giving me another option. "Can you point me in the direction of the kitchen for a snack. I didn't have dinner last night."

A little bit of regret flowed into me. Whoa, I hadn't expected that.

He ran a hand through his already messy hair. "I should've brought you something." His eyes widened in surprise, and confusion replaced it. "I mean ..."

Awkward tension wafted between us.

"So ..." I couldn't stand the silence. "Which way is the kitchen?"

"Uh ..." He pointed in the opposite direction of where Tyler and Mike, Brock's father and alpha of their pack, had been sitting last night when they'd dragged me in. "That way."

"Thanks." I walked past him, heading in that general direction.

He rushed after me. "Let me go with you."

No. God, no. "You don't need to." If I acted vehemently opposed to his company, that would only solidify his intention to join me. Whether I liked it or not, I'd have to play the game Tyler had taught me even if he hadn't meant to. "I'd hate to put you out."

"You know I have to join you." His face set into its usual arrogant countenance with his chin prominently upward, and his animosity was undeniable.

Even though I hated that he'd claimed me, I had to pretend I didn't. "Okay."

His face slipped before he could smooth it back into place.

We continued our trek down the hall. I tried to act casual as I took in every detail I could. Unlike the room they'd put me in, the hallway was a warm gray, and the flooring was a maple wood that contrasted nicely. We passed by two more doors, one on each side, before the hallway opened up into a formal living room.

An off-white tufted couch was centered in front of a glass wall overlooking the city. In the corner was a large television that could be pulled into the center of the living room. A long fireplace was built into the side wall. I'd never seen anything like it.

"Are you coming?" Brock huffed.

"Oh, yeah. Sorry." The house I'd grown up in was nice but in a traditional way. Tyler liked gaudy furniture and mountain views. I shook my head and glanced outside but couldn't find anything distinguishable. The sky was still dark. Not even the sun was awake yet.

I followed him into a large dining room with a dark cherry wood table that could seat fourteen easily. To the right was a set of white doors that likely led to the kitchen.

He opened them and surprisingly waved me through.

"Thanks." I kept ample room between us as I walked past him, not wanting to risk even brushing against him. After what happened last night, I could never trust him.

The kitchen was massive with the same maple flooring and white cabinets. A large, dark gray island stood in the center with a sink sitting in the middle and a dishwasher to the side. The refrigerator was dark steel, keeping up the ambiance.

I ran my hand along the marble island top, not sure what else to do.

Brock watched me and crossed his arms. "Are you going to eat or not?"

"Seeing as I don't know where anything is, maybe you can help me out?" I tried to keep the annoyance out of my voice but failed miserably.

He pointed to a white door behind me in the corner, which led into a large pantry. "Well, that's where the unrefrigerated food is, and there," he said, pointing to the refrigerator, "is where the cold food is. Any questions?"

I placed my hands on my hips and clenched them. For once, I enjoyed the feelings of intense dislike and anger toward Brock. I'd been scared after last night, that things would change between us. The only thing that was different was his yo-yoing emotions. "Your intellect astonishes me."

As soon as the words had left my lips, I regretted them. I was supposed to behave, not act belligerently.

Brock shut the doors, which caused his scent to become so strong it made my head swim as he marched over to me. He placed his thumb firmly under my chin, lifting my face toward him. "You need to remember I own you now. A little respect would go a long way."

"Let's be clear." He expected me to avert my eyes, so of course, I stared right into his, challenging him. "You will never own me. I'm not a piece of property you can claim and mold into what you want. I'm my own person and can stand on my own two feet."

Sweat beaded over his lip with the weight of my threat, and his chin trembled, showing he was struggling to maintain eye contact.

I hadn't meant to make him submit to me, but now that he might, I relished the feeling. If he saw me as an alpha, he'd have to listen to me. I'd make him get me the hell out of here. I wouldn't hesitate to use the alpha will on him.

"You ... will ... be ..." He strained each word out, trying to keep control.

The kitchen door opened and slammed against the wall. Tyler marched into the room. His gaze landed on me, and he frowned. "What the hell is going on here?"

Brock sighed with relief as he tore his focus from me

and regarded the alpha. "Sadie was hungry, so I showed her where the kitchen is."

"You woke him up to eat?" Disdain etched Tyler's face as he shook his head in disgust. "You should know better."

"I didn't mean to." I sounded so weak. Why did I get this way around him? "I didn't eat last night, so I wanted a snack."

"You can go back to bed." Tyler pointed his thumb at the door. "I'll stay here with her."

"Are you sure?" Brock acted like he didn't want to go. "I'm sure you need your rest too."

Correction, he was still brownnosing, thank God. Things needed to remain the same between us. Any deviation scared the shit out of me.

"I'm positive." Tyler glared at me. "I need time to talk to my *daughter* alone." His outright lie was devoid of the signature sulfuric scent. He loved flaunting the fact that he was the one shifter ever capable of lying. A little trick that his father taught him so they could rise to the top without anyone detecting their untruths.

He'd emphasized the word *daughter*, but Brock wouldn't understand or catch on. Tyler planned to use it as a weapon ... a very effective one.

"Sure." Brock nodded and avoided looking at me again. He probably didn't want to risk another stare-off. It thrilled me that I was so much stronger than him.

"See ya." I walked over to the pantry and opened the door. Each wall had three shelves brimming with food.

Brock's footsteps retreated across the living room and down the hall, leaving Tyler and me alone in the kitchen.

"You're wearing the same clothes as last night." Tyler walked over to the island and sat on a barstool. "Why do you insist on embarrassing me?"

"I got kidnapped." I snatched a bag of bagels from the shelf and joined him at the island. I opened drawers, looking for a plate, and used the opportunity to snoop for something that might hint at our location. "It's not like I have extra clothes or anything." I moved to the cabinets against the far wall.

"We made sure you'd have everything you need here." He stood and walked over to me.

I naturally tensed and stopped moving. When he got close, bad things usually went down.

His arm brushed against mine as he reached above my head and opened the cabinet. "Looking for this?" He removed a plate and handed it to me.

"Thanks." I took the plate, not happy that he'd cut my perusal short. Needing to act normal, I opened the refrigerator and found the cream cheese.

"Let me get you a knife too." He moved to the end and opened the drawer containing the silverware. "I'd hate for you to have to open up every drawer to find it." He leaned over the island and handed me the utensil.

With him here, I wouldn't be able to find a damn thing. He already knew what I was up to, and he hadn't been here five minutes. I took the knife and spread the cream cheese over my cinnamon raisin bagel.

He sat back on the stool and tapped his fingers on the counter. "I've been thinking ..."

That was his tell. He tapped his fingers before he dropped a bomb on someone. It put me on edge, but I tried to give off a calm persona. "Hmm." I placed the knife on the plate.

"A lot has happened since I last saw you." He tapped his foot on the ground. "You left my pack and hid from your own father ..." He chuckled at those words. "And you've been God knows where."

I already knew where this was going. He was goading me to see what I would do. I looked at him as I took a bite of my bagel. "And?"

"I want to know all those answers," he said simply.

"You didn't ask a question." I chewed my food slowly. My stomach grew queasy, but if I wanted to make it out of here, I'd need strength and energy.

He slammed his hand on the table. "Do not play games with me."

Everything inside me wanted to recoil, but I managed not to flinch. I took another bite of my bagel, playing with fire.

His nostrils flared. He wasn't happy with my actions. "Who is your alpha?"

"Well, there were only two options the night we left you." I placed my hands on the counter. "Roxy or me."

"Are you saying you're still her alpha?" He laughed hard. "Are you serious?"

"What did you expect?" Anger bubbled inside me. "Us to run and find another wolf shifter to pledge our loyalty to immediately?"

"You're a woman." He placed his forearms on the table. "No wonder you've fucked everything up so bad."

He wanted me to lose my cool. Instead, I picked up my bagel and ate, letting him see he wasn't affecting me.

Tyler lifted an eyebrow. "Where have you been?"

"Honestly, I'm not sure." That wasn't a lie. "It was on a mountain. I didn't drive there and couldn't get back there if I wanted to." I skirted around telling him it was the Smoky Mountains by staying vague.

"Who did you stay with?" He wouldn't let it go.

"A small nest of vampires." I had to downplay it. "It's the two vampires you tried to get to kill the two guys you tortured."

"Oh, them." His nose wrinkled. "Then how did you find out about your heritage?"

Thank God he'd moved on from that. He didn't care about them since he considered them weak. "I told you, the fae started attacking me."

"But something had to trigger it." He leaned forward. "So what did?"

This was a safe story to share with him, but I would need to edit out the parts I didn't want him to know. For instance, that it had been after my first date with Donovan. "It happened before all that crap went down with you that night. I walked into the dorm bathroom and found a teal-haired girl crying at the sink. I touched her shoulder to comfort her, and something inside me popped."

Tyler leaned back and crossed his arms. "Why were you back on campus last night?"

He asked the same questions in different ways to catch people in a lie. That was the trick I'd learned growing up: stick as close to the truth as possible so you don't have to remember all the lies. "Like I told you, the fae kept attacking, and I figured the fae girl could help."

"And did she?"

Now I had to tell him part of the truth. I'd hoped to keep it hidden, but if I lied, he'd know. "Yes, she hid my magic."

"The fae aren't a threat to all of us, then." He smirked. "I knew you were holding something back last night."

"You got me." If he thought he'd one-upped me, it would help with all the other truths I wanted to keep from him. "Is there anything else?"

"How did you know I'm not your father?" He squinted at me as the last tough question fell from his lips. "Why didn't you consider your mother was fae?"

Shit. I had to think fast on my feet. "You weren't the most loving parent." I had to choose my next words carefully.

"Well, no." He lowered his voice. "But I've killed every one of my children, so that's not what gave it away." He leaned forward. "You saw her, didn't you?"

There was no getting around this. "Yes."

When he broke into deep laughter, it shocked me. It sounded so cold and crazed.

Tears pooled at the corners of his eyes. "How did she react to her beloved daughter still being alive after all this time?"

"You're enjoying this?" My hand inched toward the butter knife. It might not do much, but maybe I could make the asshole bleed. "Does this make you feel big and powerful?"

He stood and rushed toward me. He grabbed my shoulders and shoved me into the cabinet behind me. "I am powerful. I took her daughter away from her, not once but twice."

I refused to cower and feed his ego. "It's awfully sad that you can only get off by causing others pain."

He fisted his hand, his intent clear.

I closed my eyes and waited for the pain.

CHAPTER THREE

W hen nothing happened, I opened my eyes. He rarely was physical with me, but only because he didn't want others to see me blemished.

"You see." He lowered his face to mine, so close his breath hit me in the face. "That's true power, making others cower in fear."

I breathed raggedly, hating that he'd gotten to me. "Fear and power are two different things."

"No, they aren't." His hand squeezed my shoulder. "Stupid, weak people think that. It helps them feel better about themselves."

That wasn't true, but I had no doubt he believed it. Fear had always been his tactic, and when it didn't work, he killed, instilling more fear in others.

"Sure, we'll go with that." My mouth had taken on a life of its own.

"Are you mocking me?" His jaw clenched. "I've raised you better than that."

I wanted to keep pushing him, but that wouldn't work

in my favor. Even though my wolf howled inside, I forced myself to avert my gaze. "Why are you being like this?"

"To remind you of your place." He released my shoulder and lifted his chin. "I am and will always be stronger than you. There's no point in fighting it."

There was but not right now. I had to remember my original plan—be complaisant. "Fine." I repeated the words over in my head.

"Good girl," he said condescendingly. "Now tomorrow is your mating ceremony with Brock."

Tomorrow. Being reminded of it turned my stomach. Dammit. *Donovan?* I hated to bother him if he was asleep, but I needed to know where they were and if they had located me yet.

Yes. I'm here.

My stomach sank hard. *Please tell me you're close to finding me.*

We're in Atlanta. He sounded disgusted. *But it's hard getting a good location on you with all the shit in the city. The others are sleeping, but I'm searching for you.*

Please tell me you aren't in wolf form. That would be problematic in a city like this. If he got caught, he'd be treated like a wild animal.

No. I had to shift to human form. He didn't sound thrilled. *Which is part of the problem. Did you find anything? We have to get you out of there before that ceremony.*

Not yet. Something had to give. *Tyler stopped my snooping. He's here with me now.*

I'm not resting until you're back here with me, where you belong, Donovan vowed. *I don't care what it takes, I will find you before that ceremony.*

Either way, I'll find a way out. Even if I had to die, I

refused to be mated to someone other than my fated mate, especially against my will. The condo wasn't high enough to provide a full view of the city, which was an issue. All I could see were other condo buildings with no distinguishing names.

Tyler cleared his throat and smirked. "You will look amazing and play your part, or there will be severe consequences."

"Like what?" What else could he take from me? There wasn't much left. "What in the world could you possibly have over my head?"

"Besides your life?" The threat rang between us.

"You won't do that." I didn't doubt he wanted to kill me. "You need me."

He frowned and wrinkled his nose, revealing his disgust. "That may be true, but I can make you wish you were dead."

Oh, he'd done that for years. "Well, you are trying to mate me off to Brock."

"Trying?" He snorted. "You will be mated off. After all, he claimed you already."

"And you're okay with that?" Claiming someone before the ceremony was frowned upon. The whole point of the ceremony was about showing the people in attendance that you were claiming each other of your own free will. "Doesn't that taint me?"

"Please," he scoffed. "I don't give a damn about your virtue. I care about you sealing the deal with Brock."

Wait ... "Did you put him up to that?"

"I may have suggested it." He lifted a hand and twirled it. "Or planted the idea in his head. He's still young and needs guidance."

That shouldn't have surprised me. Tyler had a way of

getting what he wanted. "Do you even care about me at all?" This might be my only chance to ask him.

He started. "God, no. Why would you even ask that? You are purely a means to an end."

And there it was. Even though I'd known this, it hurt so damn much to hear him blatantly admit it. He had absolutely no remorse. "Okay." Resolve filled me. I would end his reign and kill him with my bare hands. He'd taken everything away from me without a moment's hesitation.

"And this proves why women can't lead." He stepped back. "You get your emotions involved, looking for something that isn't there."

Let him think that and underestimate me. When I got my retribution, I'd be ridding the world of such evil.

The kitchen doors opened, and an older woman entered. Her gray hair was pulled into a ponytail, and she wore an apron over her jeans and shirt. "Oh, am I interrupting?"

Her salty human scent swirled around us.

"No." Tyler's charismatic façade slipped right back into place. "My daughter got here late last night and woke up hungry." He motioned to the bagel several feet away from me. "She was looking for breakfast."

"That's no breakfast." The lady smiled, making her crow's feet more pronounced. "I'm getting ready to cook now. Give me an hour, and there will be plenty for you to eat and keep you satisfied until lunch."

"That sounds great." She seemed so kind, and I didn't want to insult her. I didn't have an appetite to finish the bagel. "I'll just put my bagel away for later, then."

"You don't worry about a thing." She took the plate, walked to the end of the counter, and grabbed a bag. "I'll put it away. That's kind of my job. Now scoot on out of here and let me get to work."

I wanted to stay. She was the nicest person here. "Do you need any help?"

"Sadie," Tyler said sharply. "You heard her. This is her job, not yours."

I wanted to put my foot down and tell him where he could go, but I couldn't. Besides, he knew if I stayed with her, I could weasel out information on where we were. There was no way I could get out of this. "I made a mess and just wanted to help."

"You're a sweet girl." She patted my arm. "But I'm good and too set in my ways to have someone else flitting about my kitchen."

"My daughter tends to impose on people." Tyler glared at me. "We'll be getting out of your way now. Won't we, Sadie?"

I forced a smile. "Of course." I walked past her and Tyler to the doors.

As soon as we were out of the kitchen, Tyler grabbed my arm and spun me toward him. "Listen here. I want to make sure my expectations are clear." He inhaled sharply. "The next forty-eight hours better go off without a hitch. You will go to your room and make yourself presentable. You will change into an appropriate outfit, and when you come out here, you'll play your part well. Do you understand?"

If I desired a chance at snooping without him watching over me, I had to do what he asked, even if it pissed me off. I nodded. "I understand."

"Good." He let go of my arm and motioned for me to head back to my room. "This is your last chance. I can always make your life even worse."

Not wanting to be around him any longer, I hurried toward the room. I refused to call it mine.

I STARED at the reflection in the mirror and didn't recognize the girl looking back at me. I looked better than I had last night. My eyes weren't sunken, and my makeup was perfect. I even wore black designer slacks and a cute, stylish top that was almost the same rose-gold shade as my hair.

The entire day had been tedious. Tyler and Mike had gone on and on about the mating ceremony, and an event coordinator had shown up to ask final questions about the ceremony. Apparently, they'd been planning this since I'd run away so when I came back, they could get a jump-start.

The ceremony would be taking place in the condo, so I had to get a location and fast. *Please tell me you guys are closer.*

We've narrowed it down to several blocks. Donovan sounded as frustrated as I felt. *All these damn people make it hard to find anything.*

Have you had any luck? Roxy joined the conversation. *Anything that could help us narrow down your location further?*

No, but Tyler and Mike are leaving. I didn't want to state the obvious—that I'd be alone with Brock. I wasn't sure if Donovan could handle that, and I couldn't blame him. *It'll give me a chance to do more investigative work.*

If he tries something with you, kill him, Donovan growled.

I promise. There was no way I'd let Brock take anything else from me—or us. *I will.*

A knock sounded at the door.

Even if I hadn't smelled his overly musky scent, I would have known who it was. Tyler and Mike were going out to meet with business associates, and they'd made it clear they were leaving Brock and me here alone to spend some much-needed time together before the ceremony.

I wanted to gag, but Brock wasn't as smart as Tyler. If I wanted a chance at finding out something, it would be with him. I glanced at myself one last time when he knocked again and turned the doorknob.

And that was why I'd locked it. I didn't need these assholes walking in whenever they pleased.

"Sadie," he called. "Our dads are leaving."

A shiver ran down my spine. I couldn't believe I'd ever called that jackass Dad. "Coming."

Forcing myself to walk toward the door, I slid my lipstick into the pocket of my slacks while, trying to calm my already racing heart. I opened the door to find Brock leaning against the doorframe. His hair was messier than normal like he'd purposely styled it that way, and his musky smell was even more overwhelming, which I had thought was impossible.

He wore tight slacks that left little to the imagination and a button-down shirt tucked into his pants. The hem of his shirt was visible through his pants.

Dear God. Who'd dressed him?

He must have thought he looked sexy because he gave me what he considered a smoldering look. However, it reminded me of the picture he'd given me back at the dorm. The poor guy looked awkward and constipated. I wanted to say, "Maybe you should eat more veggies. I heard that helps." But I didn't.

"Hey." He leaned his head against the doorframe. "You look hot."

Tyler thought mating me off to this guy would bring him unlimited success? A laugh bubbled up my throat, but I swallowed it down ... somehow. "Hi?" It came out more like a question. "And thanks." I wasn't about to compliment him back. He'd smell the lie.

"Sadie," Tyler called from down the hall. "Come tell me goodbye."

Ever the dutiful daughter, I happily pushed past Brock and headed toward the two alphas waiting to go to the garage.

"Goodbye." A little annoyance must have coated my words because Tyler's shoulders tensed.

"You two behave," Tyler said as he pointed at me and then Brock.

"Yes." Mike chuckled as his fingers stuck into his overly gelled hair. It didn't even budge. His beady brown eyes looked at me with disdain. "We don't need any blemishes marring either one of you before the ceremony, so make sure to hide any hickeys under your clothes." He tugged at the suit jacket that swallowed his large frame.

Gag me now. That would definitely not be happening.

"Noted," Brock said as he wrapped an arm around my waist. I felt dirty.

Somehow, I stayed put even as I died a little inside.

"Well, then," Mike said and slapped Tyler on the shoulder. "Let's leave these two love birds alone."

"All right." Tyler narrowed his eyes in warning then turned and headed down the stairs. "We don't want to keep the other alphas waiting."

Brock and I stayed in place and watched as they went downstairs.

When the door shut, Brock cleared his throat and looked at me. "Are you hungry?"

"Yeah." I was starving but didn't want to eat. It was a weird cycle.

"Let's go ask Betty to make us something." He took my hand and tugged me toward the kitchen.

An idea settled over me. "They're working hard on preparations for tomorrow. I'd hate to bother them. What about a pizza instead?" I knew he had a love for pizza and could make use of it to my advantage. "I haven't had it in a while, and it sounds really good."

"A woman after my own heart." He placed a hand on his chest and led me down toward the living room.

No, I wasn't after his heart, but I sure as hell was hoping to glean an address while he placed the order.

Once we reached the room, I casually sat on the couch. "How about two with all the meats?"

"Sounds great." He pulled his phone from his pocket and grinned. "Let me go order it. I'll be right back." He turned and walked down the hallway.

As soon as he turned the corner, I jumped to my feet and ran to the edge of the room. I glanced and saw him walking down the other end of the hall and into his room across the hallway from mine.

It was risky, but I had to get closer to hear him. I tiptoed down the hallway and stopped at his door. I could now hear him in the other room.

"Yes, two pizzas, all the works." He paused, listening to the other end. "Yes, the address is 3376 Peachtree Road. Waldorf Astoria Residences, Unit 32."

Jackpot. *Guys. I've got the address.* I told them where I was, hope once again fueling me. I'd make it out of here after all.

We're on our way, Donovan replied. *We'll scope it out and get back to you.*

Brock's footsteps headed my way.

Shit, I'd zoned out after getting the address. There was no way I could hide without him catching me.

CHAPTER FOUR

His footsteps grew closer to the door, and I did the only thing I could think of. I straightened and raised my hand like I was about to knock.

The door opened, revealing a scowling Brock. "What are you doing?"

I dropped my hand and motioned to the bar. "I wanted to see if you wanted a drink." If I meant it now, it wouldn't be a lie. "I thought it might be nice."

"Oh." He licked his lips, and his brows furrowed. "That does sound nice. I could stand something strong."

"Perfect." I grinned and headed toward the bar. "There's wine, right?"

"Yeah." He caught up to me. "There's a built-in wine chiller. Mom can't go without her wine."

His mom. I'd forgotten about her. She didn't come around often. I was pretty sure she stayed away as much as possible. "Where is she? I figured she'd be here for tomorrow."

I'd only met her a handful of times, but each encounter

had been positive. She cowered around Mike, but that was the way alpha men liked to treat their women.

The few times she and I had talked alone, she'd been funny and down to earth. She'd been pressured into mating with Mike just like Mom had been with Tyler. The only difference was that Mom had been strong enough to do something about it and run away. His mother was not.

"She's back home where she should be." Brock frowned and sucked in air. "But don't worry. She'll be here first thing in the morning for our ceremony. She was over the moon when she heard we'd found you and we'd be mated soon. She likes you."

"Where she should be?" We'd only been together a few minutes, and already he'd rubbed me the wrong way. "What do you mean?"

"She has no place here when we're conducting business." He puffed his chest. "Which is what's been going on."

"Yeah. Okay." I tried to sound disinterested, but my annoyance bled through, and my mouth ran. "I guess because she doesn't have a dick, she's not very useful?"

"What would your father say if he heard you talk like that?" Brock scoffed. "You need to learn some manners and quickly."

He pushed me too far. "I don't give a flying fuck what he has to say."

"You better." Brock faced me. "As of tomorrow, you'll be a reflection on me, so get that through your head. I expect perfection."

"Good luck with that." My intense hate for him revived. "You realize Tyler isn't my alpha anymore?" I needed to take his arrogance down a notch. "I'm not part of his pack."

Brock shrugged. "It doesn't matter. You're still his blood, and blood trumps everything."

"Now that's something we can agree on." Granted, I'd learned that blood could be forged through friendships as well. My pack, Egan, Lillith, and Katherine were as much my blood as Mom and my grandparents. "But there is more than one way you can become blood."

"If I didn't know any better, I'd think you're insinuating that you don't consider Tyler your family." Brock grabbed my arm, stopping me in my tracks. "Which is not the case. You better come to terms with everything."

I entered the bar area, putting space between us. I already felt suffocated, and the bond hadn't been cemented. Even knowing it wouldn't happen didn't dampen his presence around me.

"I'll take a whiskey, neat," he said, expecting me to pour his drink.

I grabbed a wine glass and a small cup from under the cabinet and poured him a whiskey. Everything in me wanted to throw the contents of the glass in his face, but I reined in the urge ... barely.

I grabbed a pinot grigio from the chiller and poured the wine up to the brim.

"Classy," Brock grumbled. "Is this a repeat performance from the steak house?"

A giggle escaped before I could hold it back as the memory of that night flashed in my head. Brock had been set on dating me for God knew how long, and he finally decided to pursue me at Kortright. I'd agreed to go on a date with him and embarrassed the hell out of him. My goal had been for him to lose interest in me, but Brock only wanted me to show allegiance to my father and unite our families.

Tyler would gain financial backing from Brock's family, and Brock's family would rise in power.

A vein between his eyes bulged. "That wasn't meant to be funny."

"Would it make you call the ceremony off?" If it would, I'd act that way in a heartbeat, but I already knew his answer.

"No." He lifted his chin in defiance. "I've claimed you. Even if I reconsidered, I'm locked in now."

"But if you hadn't claimed—"

"Tomorrow would still be on." Brock walked in front of the bar and faced me. "Am I that horrible?"

"Are you sure you want me to answer that question?" If I lied, he'd know. My hands were tied. "You know not to ask something you don't want to know the answer to."

"Yeah, I do." Brock lifted his hands. "I've been nothing but considerate toward you."

"Really?" I handed him his drink and took a large sip of wine. "You forced me into a date you knew I didn't want."

"I ..." He stopped.

"Tyler promised me to you behind my back." I pointed at him. "That should give you a clue." I held up a third finger, counting off the reasons. "You treat my best friend like shit. You had a vampire attack and drain a human I cared for. You kidnapped me. You know I don't want to follow through with the mating ceremony, but you're still determined and bit me to force it. You're arrogant, egotistical, and treat women and anyone you consider beneath you like shit." I arched an eyebrow. "Should I keep going?"

He drained his cup and placed it back on the bar top. "No, I think I get the gist." Guilt and anger flowed off him, connecting with me.

"I warned you." I hated that I could feel him so clearly.

It was like he was a packmate, which made me wonder if he could feel me. "Why did you ask, anyway? Can't you feel my emotions?"

"No, why would you ask that?" His forehead creased, and his eyes widened. "Wait, can you feel me?"

"Ever since you bit me, yeah." I was relieved I was still cut off from him. Escaping wouldn't be as hard with him unable to read me. It made sense since I hadn't claimed him or tried to bond with him in any way. "And you have many conflicting emotions, which confuses me."

"Dammit," he growled and reached across the counter for the whiskey bottle, filling his glass once more. "That wasn't supposed to happen."

"Well, maybe you shouldn't have done it, then." I drained the rest of my wine and poured a second glass. "Sometimes, karma's a bitch."

"Tell me about it." He threw back a second glass, and silence descended between us. "Look, I don't mean to be an ass to you, but there are certain expectations of both you and me." Regret flowed through the bond. "If we don't mate tomorrow, it's not just your ass on the line. It's expected of me just as much as it's expected from you."

He had me softening toward him again. I didn't like it when I felt more than rage and hate toward him. The bond had to be messing with me. His wolf was partly connected to mine. I had to remember that. "Just because it's expected doesn't mean it's right."

"It doesn't matter." He ran his finger along the rim of his glass. "I claimed you. There's no going back."

"You do realize good ol' Tyler suggested it for a reason." Tyler manipulated everyone to get his way. That was how the asshat worked. "And it does matter. I haven't claimed you, and we haven't completed the bond." Maybe I could get him on my side.

"No," he said and met my eyes. "This will go on tomorrow."

If he wanted to command me, two could play that game. I locked my gaze with his again.

His eyes widened as if he remembered what had happened the other day. He tipped his glass, and it landed sideways on the counter.

"Oops." He broke his gaze and acted like the glass might have broken. "Okay. Good. It's fine."

I openly rolled my eyes. That was a coward's way out.

Awkward tension sprung between us, and I welcomed it, hoping he felt uncomfortable.

After a few seconds, he cleared his throat. "You said you aren't part of your dad's pack anymore, so who's your alpha now?"

The question sounded innocent and informed me that Tyler hadn't shared this little nugget of information. "Actually, I'm the alpha."

"Well, Roxy couldn't handle it, so that makes sense." He nodded. "It must be the two of you, then."

Yeah, not answering that. I took another large sip of wine. "How many people are in your pack?" I deflected, knowing it would work. It would be good to get an idea of their numbers, and he'd love to gloat since he was an arrogant ass.

"Oh, our pack has grown in the last few years." Brock relaxed and sat on a stool at the front of the bar. "We have over a hundred and fifty pack members now. We absorbed a few more packs recently."

More like a hostile takeover. That was exactly how Tyler grew his own pack. "Wow."

"We're the biggest pack, other than Tyler's." Brock was growing excited. "And when we have our boy, he'll be the future leader over both packs. It'll set us up to do so much."

He meant control so much. "You know, boys aren't guaranteed."

"We'll have one," he said determinedly, like he could force his will on nature. "I don't care how many times we have to try."

Great. That sounded like so much fun. I'd learned from all my years with Tyler that saying nothing was sometimes the best strategy, so I focused on my wine.

Brock's phone rang, diffusing the entire awkward conversation.

He answered it. "Okay. I'm on my way down." He looked at me. "The pizza is here. Don't go anywhere. I'll be right back."

As he walked away, I knew my plans for the rest of the night: eat, don't talk, and convince him to play pool so I could leave something down there I would need later. That shouldn't be too bad.

THE NIGHT HAD GONE by slowly even though I'd made it back into my room by eight. I'd spent over two hours with Brock, and that solidified that I could never spend the rest of my life with him. Not that it was even a question.

Any update? I'd drunk heavily the entire time with him. Even though I wasn't drunk, I had a good buzz, but I needed something to get me through the night. *Please tell me you have good news.*

We're right outside. Donovan sounded as flustered as I

felt. *There are at least twenty wolf shifters hanging outside. I'm not sure how the hell we're going to get you out.*

I didn't want to spend another night here, but I didn't see another option. *We'll need to use the ceremony as a distraction.* That was our best bet.

No. Donovan sounded resolved. *We're getting you out tonight.*

Look, I want her here as badly as you, Roxy interjected. *But Sadie has a point. Knowing Tyler and Mike, this will be a huge event, which means a ton of people coming in and out. It'll be easier for her to slip out that way.*

That's cutting it too close. Donovan's anger coursed through the pack bond. *I won't risk it.*

Man, Axel said slowly to his best friend. *Trying to get her out now will get us all caught, which means she'll have to go through with the ceremony tomorrow.*

I felt my mate's turmoil and linked only to him. *The ceremony starts at noon, which means between getting everything set up and people arriving, it's going to be a whirlwind. This is our best chance.*

Are you sure you want to leave? Insecurity gripped him.

Normally, I'd be pissed, but he needed understanding right now. *Of course, I want to leave. That's the whole point. You heard Roxy and Axel. They agree with me. You should know better than to even ask this.*

Because I've been wanting to complete the mate bond ever since I turned into a wolf. His voice lowered. *And you kept telling me you wanted to wait.*

Remember how volatile you were when you first turned wolf? It wrecked me that he thought I didn't want to complete the bond. *I didn't want to do anything to heighten your wolf even more until you'd acclimated. Do you not remember what we were doing before the last fae attack?*

He'd almost claimed me. If the fae had waited a few seconds longer, he would've. *You are it for me.*

I'm sorry. He sighed. *I'm being stupid. Not having you here is driving me insane.*

And being stuck here is hurting me too. He had to know how much I cared. *I love you. Hell, those words don't even capture what I feel for you.*

I love you too, he growled again. *And tomorrow, if you don't get out on your own, I'm coming in to get you.*

I opened the link back up to everyone. *Do you see a garage?*

Yes, we're driving by it now, Donovan answered. *Why?*

That's my exit. It was the only place that made sense now that I'd thought about it. *Everyone is focused on the other side of the condo. The kitchen staff is crazy right now.*

Okay, sounds like a plan, Axel agreed. *I guess all we can do is get some rest and prepare for tomorrow.*

Yes, and make sure Mom and Titan stay out of sight. The last thing I needed was for Tyler to figure out where Mom was and search for their pack. *If they get spotted, it could compromise our location.*

Noted, Donovan said with resolve. *We'll keep them in the car like last time. Katherine and Lillith can help instead.*

I'm going to change and try to get some sleep. I probably wouldn't have much luck, but I needed to be on full alert in the morning. *I'll get up early again, and the first chance I have to sneak out, I'll take it. I'm hoping I can get out before the first guests arrive since Mike and Tyler went out with some pack alphas. They usually use wolfsbane to get drunk.*

We'll be here by four in the morning, Donovan stated. *I don't want us to miss an opportunity for your escape.*

Ugh, Roxy whined. *If this doesn't prove how much I love you, nothing will.*

I laughed, knowing how much she hated mornings. *I love you too.* I headed to the shower, needing some time alone.

The warm water melted away some of my stress, but not all of it. Tomorrow would be a big day with no room for error. I refused to let Tyler dictate my life any longer. I only hoped we didn't run into any issues, but things usually didn't go in my favor.

CHAPTER FIVE

As expected, I couldn't fall asleep even in the heavenly bed. The room might have been gouge-your-eyes-out white, but the bed was the equivalent of lying on a cloud. It was the only bright spot in this godforsaken place.

Commotion came from down the hall toward the basement, indicating that Mike and Tyler were home.

"He has to know he doesn't have a choice." Tyler's slurred words echoed down the hallway. "He will submit to me one way or another. His pack will be mine."

Yup, he was plastered. Otherwise, he wouldn't be speaking so loudly. He always enhanced his drink with wolfsbane, but he rarely let himself lose control unless someone had infuriated him.

"Did you not see how nervous he was?" Mike chuckled and sounded as plastered as Tyler. "He knows it. He's just trying desperately to retain control. You know it's hard for an alpha to hand over his pack."

I figured that was why they'd gone out tonight. Tyler enjoyed conquests more than anything.

"As soon as Brock and Sadie conclude their ceremony,

we'll take him down in front of everyone," Tyler said with enthusiasm. "Had he shown more respect and compliance tonight in front of the others, I would've done it more privately. But he has to know I'm the one in charge ... always and forever."

Further proof that the mating ceremony was about him gaining more power.

"And you'll always have my backing," Mike vowed. "It's a blessing that we have kids the same age so we can tie our families together in the only way that matters."

I dry-heaved. That was how bad it sounded. They'd been scheming for longer than I'd realized. Was that another reason he'd wanted to keep me? To mate me off to that family?

"Yes, it was quite perfect." Tyler's voice grew louder as they came closer to my room. "After you proved your loyalty to me instead of Titan all those years ago and helped me kill the Hermunslie pack's alpha and beta's family, it's the least I can do. If Titan and the Hermunslie packs had stood together, they would have had too much influence. The fact that Titan ran off after his best friend died made the victory even sweeter, and good riddance. They can stay up there on that mountain and freeze for all I care."

At least, he wasn't interested in finding Titan.

"I still can't believe that Hermunslie's grandson attended Kortright." Mike laughed loudly. "That pack was way too strong for their own good. Strong alphas should never mate with humans, and they were getting up there in age anyways so they deserved what they got. It was damn lucky you found their grandson at Kortright even though he was banging Sadie. Between their grandson and the beta's grandson attending Kortright together, it was like fate had led them back to us to finish the cycle. I thought we'd killed all the kids in the attack back then. Someone must have snuck them out."

They had to be talking about Donovan and Axel. Was that what had happened? His grandparents and parents had stood with Titan, and Tyler and Mike had slaughtered them. That would make sense since Torak had recognized Axel's smell. Maybe they'd been around each other as babies.

"Well, I thought that vampire took care of them," Tyler said proudly. "Even though her death was problematic. She could've helped secure the vampire vote from all the children she created." He sounded disgusted as he continued. "If my daughter had secured the dragon and convinced him to align with me, that never would've happened. Not to mention that when she got here, she still smelled like that half-breed."

Egan never would've worked with them. He had morals and a strong code of ethics. From what I'd heard, dragons were power-hungry, but everything I'd learned about Egan was the opposite. He felt protective over the weak and would never exploit them like Tyler.

"Don't worry." Mike stopped right outside my door. "Brock will get a handle on her. A girl like her needs a firm mate by her side to remind her of her place. You did excellent in raising her for how busy you were. I'll make sure Brock focuses on her and turns her into the lady we all need her to be."

In other words, Tyler had a pass because he'd always been on the road and not around. Maybe it'd been a blessing. My entire childhood, I'd prayed he would come home and take me to the zoo or for a run in the woods. I'd wanted a father. Now, I was thankful my prayers hadn't been answered.

"I have no doubt." Tyler yawned. "Between the three of us, we'll break her spirit. I refuse to allow her to become like her mother."

"Yes, that woman was gorgeous but too strong for her own good," Mike said with disgust. "And she filled Christie's head with dangerous ideas."

I could only imagine what they were insinuating. Maybe she had an opinion on pack matters or wanted to have a say in their child's education.

"Speaking of Christie." Tyler paused. "We should get to bed. We have a big day tomorrow."

"That we do," Mike agreed. "And the living room will be packed. I'm thinking we'll have at least fifty of our closest allies and friends."

Please, they didn't have any friends, only people who were under their thumb.

My breathing evened out as they moved away from my door. My mind raced with all of the brand-new information. I wasn't sure how that information would affect my relationship with Donovan and Axel, but now wasn't the time to think about it.

Any hope of sleep vanished. I threw the covers off me and sat in bed. The clock on the nightstand glowed three in the morning. Apparently, those two weren't worried about looking hungover for the ceremony, but it meant that they should fall asleep quickly and deeply. All I needed to do was give them time to get settled in bed and close their eyes.

I climbed to my feet and paced the wide-open area in front of the bed. It was the only thing I could think of to do to get rid of all of my nervous energy so I wouldn't do anything foolish when I tried to escape.

Sadie, are you up? Donovan's voice popped into my head. *We're heading that way.*

I started and glanced at the clock again. It was now a few minutes after four. I'd lost track of time. *Yes, I'm up.*

Okay, good. Donovan's excitement penetrated the bond. *I'm so ready to get you out of there.*

Same. If I had to be around those three much longer, I might stab my eyes out. *How long until you're here?* Now that they were officially heading this way, I was ready to get the hell out.

We should be there in five minutes.

Then I'm going to try to get into the basement where the garage is. The earlier the better. Most of the guards were sleeping since they'd need extra eyes during the ceremony. With enemies like theirs, I'd bet that at least one person would try to crash.

Okay, but be safe. Donovan sounded worried. *Do whatever you have to so Tyler isn't alerted.*

They were out drinking and got back about an hour ago. A chill ran through me as their conversation came back to mind. *I doubt he'll hear me. I want to sneak out while they're dead to the world.*

We're almost there. Roxy joined the conversation. *Go ahead. If you need help, just yell.*

You don't even know where I am. This place was huge. I'd seen the view outside the window, and if we were connected to a hotel, it meant it was even more massive.

We can figure it out even if we have to get Egan to fly to all the windows, Roxy retorted. *We're all antsy to get you back here.*

Fine. I'll concentrate on getting out of here. I shut down the link and focused on my surroundings. I couldn't do what I'd done last night with Brock. He'd almost caught me sneaking out the door because I'd been wrapped up in talking with them.

I put on yoga pants and a comfortable shirt that didn't restrict my movements. At the door, I paused and took a deep breath. Once I opened that door, there'd be no going back, no matter what happened.

Placing my ear on the door, I tapped into my wolf to enhance my hearing. I could hear people at the end of the house toward the kitchen. I felt bad for Betty and her crew. They'd been working nonstop to make sure everything was perfect.

Confirming there were no noises close by, I slowly opened the door and stepped into the hallway, looking both ways.

The coast was clear.

My heart pounded in my ears as I turned toward the stairs. I walked slower than I wanted to, being extra careful so the floor didn't creak. One little sound could alert anyone nearby that I was out of my room.

The minutes crawled by as I crept down the hall. Everything in me told me to run, but it would increase my chances of getting caught. Besides, Brock was in a bedroom right across the hall. I'd rather deal with a guard than his sorry ass.

It was a complicated dance—moving slowly while acting casual in case someone crossed my path.

Not soon enough, I came closer to the bar area where the television sat. I heard voices coming from down the stairs, and it sounded like they were heading my way.

"Man, I hate that we won't get to see the ceremony," a guy with a deep voice said as he climbed the stairs. "I bet it's going to be epic."

"Wait until I tell everyone that you want to attend a mating ceremony," a guy with a higher-pitched voice responded. "You'll never live it down."

"Oh, shut up," the deeper voice growled. "If Mike or Tyler asked you to attend, you'd jump at the opportunity."

"Hell yeah, I would." The guy lowered his voice like that would make a difference. "I don't want to get on either of their bad sides. You saw what happened to Diego."

"Man, Diego was a dumbass." The deeper voice sounded strained. "He knew better than to tip off that pack that they were going to attempt a takeover. Hell, Tyler's family knows every one of the packs' secrets."

That had been the whole point of Tyler's father and great grandfather becoming architects. They'd built every supernatural neighborhood and kept the blueprints. There were only a handful that they hadn't built, much to their displeasure.

I glanced around for a place to hide, but it was futile. Even if I found a spot, they'd smell me. That meant there was only one way I could pull this off.

I walked over to the bar and grabbed a glass like I was pouring a drink.

The two large men stepped into the living room, and both sets of eyes landed directly on me.

"What are you doing up?" the one with the deeper voice asked.

I almost laughed because he was the taller and thinner one of the two. I would've pegged him as having the higher voice.

"Nerves." I lifted a bottle of rum and poured some into a glass. "I need something to help me calm down."

"Isn't the man supposed to be having issues the night before?" the stocky one asked in his nasally voice.

"Maybe." I shrugged casually. The last thing I wanted to do was drink it, but I had to convince them. I steeled my stomach and downed the shot, feeling the burn run down my chest. "This is my first ceremony, so it's not like I'm an expert or anything."

"Well, you got your drink," the short, burly one said. "Now, let's get you back to your room."

There went every hope of this being easy. "I'll be there in a minute." I poured another shot, more for courage than nerves.

"That wasn't a request," the taller one stated, his jaw set. "Time's up. We have it on good authority that you aren't supposed to be out of your room."

That didn't surprise me. "I'm not causing any problems." I downed another shot and hoped it would change my current situation.

It did not.

The taller one took a step toward me. "Don't make me get Tyler or Mike."

Of course, that was when Brock's overly musky smell hit my nose.

Brock rounded the corner, wearing matching pajama pants and a shirt. They were flannel, and he could almost pass for a kid. "What's going on here?"

The shorter one pointed his finger at me. "Your future mate is gallivanting around."

"*Gallivanting* is kind of a strong word." Brock turned his dark eyes on me. "Even though I don't approve of her drinking this early in the morning."

"Does it help that I haven't fallen asleep yet?" I cringed right as the last word left my mouth. That probably hadn't been the smartest thing to say.

The corner of his lips turned downward. "No, it doesn't."

"I'm sorry." I hated to do this, but I walked over to him and placed my hand on his chest. "Everything I need to do keeps running through my head, and I thought a drink would help."

"Uh ..." His forehead lined with confusion. "Well, don't get too stressed. All you have to do is make sure you're presentable."

"Oh, crap." I tilted my head back. "My lipstick. I left it downstairs."

"You can get it later." He placed his hand on mine and forced a smile. "You need some sleep."

"No, I need it. It's my favorite one. Let me run down and get it. I'll be right back."

"Maybe one of us should go with her." The taller one narrowed his eyes at me. "It's not far anyway."

"No, I'll go with her." Brock waved the other two off. "Go ahead and do your hourly checks. We were playing pool earlier, so it won't take long."

They both wanted to complain, but Brock lifted his chin, daring them to argue.

"Of course." The taller one bowed his head slightly. "We'll be on our way."

I watched the two of them walk off down the hallway, and I almost wanted to beg one of them to come back and go with me. The last person I wanted to accompany me downstairs was Brock. It had been awkward enough earlier when I'd been acting nice and he'd kept trying to kiss me.

"Come on," he said as he grinned at me.

My heart dropped into my stomach, but resolve settled inside me. I was getting out of here one way or another, even if I had to hurt the alpha heir.

CHAPTER SIX

I followed Brock down the stairs, steeling myself for the inevitable. There wouldn't be an easy way out of this. I could make him submit to me—I almost had the other day—but it might backfire. The less risky move would be to knock his ass out and run.

If I didn't calm myself, he'd either realize I was up to something or hope for something. Either option didn't bode well for me.

We entered the basement, and Brock turned to me.

His eyes settled on my lips. "I'm glad your voice woke me." He reached for my face. "In less than twelve hours, we'll be solidifying our bond." Anticipation flowed off him and into me.

Nope, not happening. I stepped back and cringed when his face dropped. I had to salvage the moment. I wasn't close enough to the door yet. "Why ruin the build-up?"

"Good point." He pursed his lips. "It'll be the last first time we'll ever have again."

"What?" My brain hadn't kept up. "I'm not following you."

"I mean, it'll be our first time together." He took a step closer to me. "And there won't be anyone else after that, so it'll be our last first time."

Oh, dear God. He planned on being faithful to me. That shocked me. Tyler and, from what I'd heard, Mike slept around. "Really?"

"Look, as long as you scratch my itch whenever I want it, there won't be a problem." He perused my body from top to bottom. "You're hot, and no one has ever intrigued me like you. And if you ever consider sleeping with someone else, I'll kill him."

Wow. Did he actually think he was being romantic? "So even if I'm not in the mood, I should force myself if that's what you want?"

"I am an alpha, and I have needs." He lifted a brow. "Surely you understand that. After all, the alpha mate is there to make sure he gets whatever he needs."

And now we were talking about each other in third person. Great. For once, I didn't have anything to say. I walked past him, making sure I didn't touch him.

He walked close behind me, not letting me get far away.

Maybe he had an inkling that something was going to happen, but he wasn't feeling anything negative. Him biting me was coming in handy.

I slowly walked over to the pool table like I didn't have a care in the world. I'd purposely left the lipstick on the side closest to the door, but it was still a good ten feet away. I needed to stun him and get the hell out of here.

My gaze landed on an alarm pad. The red light indicated it was armed. Shit, I couldn't get out of here without alerting the whole damn place. But if I could get out of the door without Brock, I'd have a little lead time, unless there were guards out front. *Hey, are you guys here?*

Yes, Donovan answered. *How are things? Are you out?*

I don't see this going smoothly. I'd hoped it would, but that probably had been officially eliminated. *Brock is down here with me. The alarm is set, and I don't know the code. Tyler will be alerted when I run.*

At least, we know ahead of time. Donovan paused for a second. *Egan and I will run across the street when the alarm goes off. Do you have any idea which floor you'll come out on?*

No. I hated being so useless. I didn't have a damn clue about anything. *The bag was over my head when I arrived.*

Roxy growled through the bond, *Those assholes are going down.*

We need to keep a level head, Axel reminded us. *If we get too upset or aggravated, more of us might get caught, and that's something none of us want.*

The truth of his words hit me hard. *All right. I'll tell you when I'm heading to the door.*

I strode over to the end of the pool table and picked up the lipstick. "Crisis averted."

"I'm sure your world would've ended if you hadn't been able to use it," Brock said condescendingly. "But I'm thankful that you've realized your appearance and how you present yourself are important. There's no room for error now that you'll be an official alpha mate."

"You mean alpha heir." I couldn't let him get away with that. He was making himself sound more important than he actually was. "You won't be alpha until your dad dies or steps down." Yeah, I might have dug the knife in deeper.

He marched over to me as fear penetrated the bond. "You will treat me with respect."

He must have realized that respect was something I couldn't give him. "You haven't done anything to earn it." I would blind him with anger and hopefully stun him when I attacked.

"With you becoming my mate, I have earned it." Brock lifted his chin, anger etched into every crevice of his face. "You should be flattered that I even want you with ..." He trailed off.

"With my freaky hair?" I assumed that was where he'd been going based on Tyler's little revelation the other day. "Thank God you're willing to do me a favor." I laughed hard. "And you wonder why I don't respect you."

"In the past, you've usually been at least agreeable." Brock's nose wrinkled. "But then you went to Kortright and made weak friends, and now you've become entitled."

"Entitled?" I backed up, purposefully getting closer to the door. "You mean demand basic rights as a wolf shifter?" A few more steps, and I'd be in a better position.

He grabbed me by the shoulders and pulled me against his chest. "Your attitude ends now. Everything changes from this moment on. Do you understand?"

He had no clue how right he was. "I completely understand."

I kneed him in the crotch, and he fell to the ground.

"What the ..." he groaned in pain, clutching his jewels.

If he thought that was bad, he'd be surprised. I kicked him in the face, and his head snapped back as blood poured from his nose.

"You're ..." he moaned as one hand stayed on his balls and the other went to his injured nose. "... gonna ..."

Footsteps pounded across the floor overhead.

Shit, he'd called the guards. I didn't know why, but I hadn't expected him to call them. They'd see how I'd beaten him up. I'd figured his pride would get in his way. Obviously, I'd been wrong.

I turned on my heel and raced to the door. I unlocked the deadbolt and heard him groaning behind me like he was trying to stand.

I yanked the door open and raced out as the alarm blared. *I'm on my way.* I entered a long hallway that led to several other condominiums. This had to be the way to the garage. *I'm not out to the garage yet. I'm running down a hallway.* Had I known that neighbors could have potentially heard my screams when they'd brought me in, I might have pitched a bigger fit.

We can hear that, Donovan stressed. *You were supposed to warn us so we'd already be racing to meet you.*

Well, sorry. My voice conveyed that I wasn't at all. *But Brock followed me down here, and our conversation went sideways. He called the guards and is limping after me.*

I ran to the double glass doors that led into the garage. The door behind me opened, and Brock stumbled out, chasing after me.

"Get your ass back here now." His voice lowered, revealing how much pain he was in. "The guards will be here soon to put you in your damn place."

Not bothering to waste time and respond, I ran out the door and tapped into my wolf. I pushed myself as hard as I could. *I'm in the garage.* The column had a large G painted on it. *And I'm on the ground floor, so I'm thinking that's the first level.*

Good. Donovan's relief was palpable. *We're running into the garage now.*

Do you see any guards? I only hoped they weren't coming in from both directions. We'd wind up in a fight sandwich. I had a feeling the risk of humans seeing didn't matter at this point.

Brock stumbled behind me, falling farther and farther

behind. He wouldn't be in pain much longer, so I needed to gain as much distance as possible.

The double doors opened again, and ten shifters raced into the garage, pursuing me.

"Stop right now!" one yelled, and then the sound of a gunshot echoed against the wall.

The air hummed as a bullet headed toward me. I'd never thought I'd ever be shot at, but in the last two months, I'd been shot at twice. I ran to the left, and the fae magic inside me rattled against the chains Naida had placed around it. The bullet breezed past me, narrowly missing my arm. *They've got guns.*

I'm going to kill them, one by one, Roxy chanted over and over like that made it better.

My heart stopped when Donovan and Egan came into view. My gaze landed on Donovan, and it was like I was seeing him for the first time again. His shaggy, jet-black hair seemed longer, and his dark blue eyes penetrated my soul. Standing next to Egan's large-ass over-seven-foot frame, he looked much smaller than his six feet three inches, but the indentions of his muscles were visible, making it clear how strong he was.

It sounded stupid. It'd only been three days, but it felt like a lifetime. I almost stopped in my tracks to take in the sight, but another gunshot sounded behind me, bringing me back down to earth.

Get down! Donovan yelled through the bond.

My magic strained against the chains, shaking them until they cracked in a few places. No, this would have all been for nothing if I let my magic out again. I needed to keep it together, even if it killed me. I couldn't let anything happen to those I loved, and I refused to be mated off to a dickwad.

I dropped to the ground as Egan's golden eyes glowed bright and his pupils turned into slits. They were only ten feet away. Egan's shirt ripped, alerting me that he was half shifting. His wings appeared behind him, and he took flight, heading straight toward me.

His huge form flew past me as his long, upward-styled blond hair blew in the breeze and dark green scales appeared over his body. The blond scruff on his chin was longer than normal, but it disappeared as the scales covered his face. His slightly accented words hit me as he growled, "Get to Donovan now."

"That's a fucking dragon!" a guard yelled.

Multiple gunshots went off, and I turned around in horror.

I couldn't let one of my best friends die for me. That wasn't how this worked. But what I saw blew my mind.

He dodged each bullet like they were nothing.

Donovan reached me and stopped.

What are you doing? I turned to see what had caught his attention. *We've got to go.*

Head on out. Donovan's eyes locked on Brock. *I'll be there soon.*

Unadulterated anger slammed into me from Brock. The alpha heir yelled, "How the hell is he alive?" He growled low, "Guards, kill him."

No. I grabbed Donovan's arm and forced him to face me. *Don't be stupid. Egan is fighting them off. We leave now. Together.*

I can't let him get away with what he did. Donovan's breathing turned rapid. *He bit you against your will.*

He just painted a target on your back by alerting the guards. If you go, I go. I refused to leave his side. *I'm not spending any more time apart.* Maybe if I played it that way, he'd come around.

He must have felt that I meant it through our bond because he paused. He raised his middle finger up to Brock. *Fine.* He spun around and faced the exit. *Let's get you out of here.*

Screams filled the air as Egan fought three shifters at the same time. Egan punched one in the face, and the guard collapsed, out cold. He grabbed the last two by their shirts and threw them all the way across the garage. They landed on two different vehicles, setting off the alarms.

He was purposely making a lot of noise so humans would come out to see what the commotion was and maybe call the cops. The only problem was it alerted more shifters too.

The other seven ran straight toward me. Brock's disappearance spoke volumes. The coward had run, leaving his guards to fight for him.

We've got to go. I tugged on Donovan. *Come on before more come out.*

The two of us ran for the exit, staying close to the cars in case they started shooting again.

The flapping of wings informed me that Egan was heading back in our direction, but more pained groans confirmed that Egan was still fighting, taking a few guards down at a time. He had the advantage since they were more worried about catching me.

I could see where the driveway dipped to the main road. Maybe we'd get out of this after all.

Another gun fired, and the bullet hit the ground right at my feet. Donovan and I dove for cover behind a red Porsche.

Egan roared, and a sickening crack sounded.

"Holy shit. He broke his neck." A guard sounded petrified. "We're all going to die."

Good, maybe they'd all freak out and run away like Brock. I'd be thrilled if they cowered in fear. They were mostly innocent and doing their jobs. Either way, they wouldn't go back without me. They'd meet certain death by Tyler's hands if they did.

A howl from back in the garage cried out as more guards came out after us. They'd rallied all the guards they had and would stop at nothing to get me.

Donovan took my hand and helped me to my feet. He said, "Come on." He glanced back at the guards and motioned for me to follow. "They're regrouping."

I took off and ran faster than I ever had in human form. Donovan kept up beside me, and soon, Egan flew on my other side.

Guys. Axel linked with the pack. *We've got a problem.*

I needed him to be specific. *What's wrong?*

Twenty guards are running this way.

The street came into view, and Axel stood right in the center of the garage opening. His brown eyes were locked on the front of the condo. He ran a hand through his short brown hair.

"Dammit," Egan rasped.

Tyler and Mike had sent every single guard after us, and they were only thirty feet away.

CHAPTER SEVEN

The magnitude of the situation hit me. If the guards reached us, we'd have no chance of getting out of here.

A few humans were on the street, so Egan couldn't take flight. We'd have to fight in our human forms.

Roxy rushed over to Axel and waved us on. Her long, flaming-red hair might as well have been a target. Her hazel eyes landed on me as she linked with the pack. *Run. The others are bringing the cars around so we can jump in.* She turned and ran in the opposite direction from the guards.

At least, we had somewhat of a plan.

The three of us pushed ourselves harder as the humans gawked. I could only imagine what they were thinking.

The guards closed in as we ran down the driveway. I wished there had been trees that could hide us or provide cover. All that surrounded us was cement and brick. I hated being in the city. Even though Tyler had an apartment in downtown Nashville, I'd always chosen to stay on the outskirts in the pack neighborhood. Wolves weren't meant to live in places like this.

We reached the sidewalk, turned right, and ran behind Roxy and Axel. They weren't far ahead since they'd waited on us, but the guards were on our tail, only fifteen feet back.

At least they weren't shooting at us with humans around. We were already making a big enough scene as it was.

The sun peeked over the horizon, spilling early morning light around us. The five of us passed by a human who was out for a run, but he came to a dead stop when he saw the guards rushing at him. He spun around and tried to keep up with us, but we left him behind.

We were running too fast to be around humans, but this was life or death. Caring would only get us hurt.

The poor guy yelled as the guards overtook him and focused on catching us.

Two cars squealed onto the road ahead of us. I hoped it was Mom and the others rescuing us, but they sounded half a mile away.

We caught up to Roxy and Axel. But once we did, Roxy fell behind, and Axel and I refused to leave her.

Go, Roxy commanded through the bond. *If they catch you, there won't be another chance for you to escape.*

And if they catch you, they'll use you as leverage, I countered. *There's no way in hell I'm leaving you behind.*

I glanced at Egan. He was the only one who couldn't communicate with us through our pack link. "Roxy can't go faster. We need to hold them off or fight them so we can all get into the cars." Now that I wasn't using all of my energy to run, I turned around and saw Lillith's van and the car speeding toward us. They were only a hundred yards away, but not close enough. The guards were gaining ground too quickly.

The cars squealed to a stop a few feet ahead of us as the

first three guards reached us. One pushed Roxy hard to the ground and lunged at me.

Arms wrapped around my waist and pushed me forward. I landed on my knees hard, and pain exploded throughout my body.

Other grunts and groans surrounded me as our group was attacked.

The guard placed all his weight on me, forcing me to the ground. As my body crumpled, I used every ounce of strength I had to roll and force the guard onto his back. His grasp around my waist didn't slacken. He wouldn't let go without a huge fight.

Facing the sky with my back plastered to his chest, I rammed my elbow in the guy's side as hard as possible.

"Ugh," he grunted, and his hold slackened.

That was all I needed. I sat up and pushed all my weight into the guy's waist. I jumped to my feet and got into a fighting stance.

"You bitch," he growled and climbed to his feet.

Foolishly, I looked around and saw that we were greatly outnumbered. Egan was struggling as well since he couldn't shift, even partially, into his dragon. He was still stronger than all of us combined, and the guards knew it, too, since ten were attacking him at once.

A car door opened, and I turned to see Mom getting out of the car. No, we couldn't allow that to happen.

My magic surged inside me, banging against the chains that bound them. Even though I hadn't meant to do it, the chains disintegrated, and my magic spilled throughout my body. The familiar static electricity mixed with my blood.

I hated that it had crumbled, but this might be our only chance to get out of this alive. I allowed my anger and emotions to guide it. It seemed to be the only time I could control it.

Three guards jumped on Egan's back, and one punched him repeatedly. How he kept standing was beyond me.

Donovan dropped to the ground as two shifters attacked, a guard had Roxy's arms locked behind her back as he dragged her toward the condo.

"Roxy!" Axel cried, but a guard punched him in the stomach.

To make matters worse, Mom stood in plain view. If Tyler saw her, she'd be a target as well.

A hand fisted into my hair and jerked my head back.

"Stupid girl," the guard rasped in my ear. "You never turn your back on your opponent."

That was the golden rule, but my world was crashing around me. I had to see it all to fuel the power inside me. The static increased to levels I'd never felt before. It felt like I might explode.

His other hand grabbed my arm, but he cried in pain and jerked his hand back. "What the hell?" He shook his hand as if to cool it off. "How did you shock me?"

"I'm part fae!" I screamed, wanting all to hear as I blasted him. He landed on his back. Hard.

Screw Tyler. Let them see I was a mutt and not a full-blooded wolf shifter. They'd seen my mother pregnant, so they'd know I'd never been his true daughter. Yes, they might not believe me if I told them, but they couldn't unsee the truth.

"Get back in the damn car!" I yelled at Mom. "You'll only make things worse."

It shocked me when she jumped back in without arguing or flat-out ignoring me, but I wouldn't question it.

I rushed over to Donovan and realized the humans had

run away. They had to be scared shitless. I didn't blame them.

The fact that I could use my magic would come in handy. My palms began to burn right when I reached Donovan. The friction didn't hurt, but the discomfort almost overwhelmed me. Two pink beams shot from my hands and hit the two guards hard in the chest. They fell, and their heads smacked the concrete, knocking them out.

"What the...?" Donovan stuttered as he stared at me with an unreadable expression.

He looked afraid, which hurt, but I couldn't read into it. I had to stay focused. "Get Roxy, and help Axel."

I spun to help the poor dragon shifter. Blood coated his face, and deep marks marred his skin from the shifters' knuckles. They were enjoying taking down a dragon despite the unconscious men on the ground. It didn't matter that there were only four of them left to do it.

The magic still raged inside me. When it didn't shoot from my palms again, I grabbed the guard who was punching my friend by the neck.

"Ah!" The guard stumbled back and faced me.

I decided to return the favor on Egan's behalf and punched the guy in his face. When my hand connected with his skin, it sizzled, and the smell of burning flesh filled my nose, making me gag.

Clutching his face, the guard stumbled away from me.

I was reaching for one of the three men on Egan's back when pink magic exploded from my hand again. It hit a guard right in the face, and he dropped to the ground.

That was all Egan needed to regain control of the situation. He had the other two guards flipped over his body and on their backs within seconds.

I glanced back at the rest of my friends. More guards

were heading our way with Tyler, Mike, and Brock running behind them.

Of course they'd be behind them. There was no way they'd be willing to risk their lives like the others were. It was sickening. What kind of leader put his people at risk while hiding? They were cowards who didn't deserve to rule.

The energy under my skin grew stronger, and my body felt on edge.

"Her eyes ..." A guard in front stopped, and the others behind him paused.

Roxy and Axel ran past me as Donovan grabbed my arm but immediately dropped it.

Come on, Donovan said and glanced back at the others. *Let's go while you have them off guard.*

But it was like I couldn't hear him. My anger raged.

"We need to go." Egan rushed toward us and glanced over his shoulder. "We need to move while they're stunned."

"She won't budge, and when I touched her, it burned." Donovan groaned in pain as he pulled harder, but nothing happened. "I don't know ..."

"It's her magic," Egan said. He bent down and picked me up. "Let's go."

The energy still charged through me, so I wasn't sure how Egan didn't get burned like the others. Maybe it was because his magic had a fae-like quality. I tried to pull it inward, but I couldn't. I was at its mercy.

Donovan ran to the older Honda Accord that Mom was in and threw open the back door. "Here."

He moved out of the way, and Egan lowered me into the car. When he pulled back, I noticed the burns on his neck from where my head had lain. I'd burned him like the guards, but he hadn't dropped me, and he'd stayed gentle with me. There was so much we didn't know about that dragon.

Tyler's yell echoed against the concrete. "Get Sadie! What the hell are you guys doing?"

The other backseat door opened, and Donovan jumped in.

"Go," Egan commanded and slammed the door.

"Wait," I said and managed to sit up to look out the back window. Egan raced to the van right behind us. Apparently, Roxy and Axel had already gotten in, and the back driver-side door was open. It was a godsend since it was on the opposite side from the guards.

As Egan reached the van, two equally horrible things happened. The guards closed in on my friend, and nearby sirens blared. The police were coming, and the last thing we needed was to be here when they arrived.

Titan shoved the car into drive, and the tires squealed as he peeled out onto the road.

I watched in horror as a guard pulled a gun on Egan, and another one pointed theirs at our car. No, we were too close. Both guns fired, and time moved in slow motion. My eyes closed as the magic inside me strobed. When I opened my eyes, both bullets had stopped just like that day when the vampire had shot at me in the woods.

Egan jumped in the van unharmed, and the bullet heading toward our car fell to the ground. Titan took a hard turn, and we raced away to safety with the van following close behind.

The next few minutes passed in silence. Now that I was here, I wasn't sure what to say or do.

"Are you okay?" Donovan asked. He touched my arm and jerked back. "Ow."

"I'm sorry." My body still felt like it was on fire. I'd lost all control. "I don't know what's happening."

Brock's intense rage filtered inside me, adding to my own. I shut our link down hard and fast, never wanting to connect with the bastard again.

"Honey." Mom turned in her seat. Her blonde hair lay limp around her face, and dark circles lined her light blue eyes that matched my own. "You need to take deep, calming breaths. It's your fae magic."

"Which means going to the university and getting caught was pointless." All that drama had been for nothing. "I didn't mean for it to happen."

Titan used the rearview mirror to look at me. His forest green eyes locked with mine as he scratched his full goatee that matched his brown hair. "If you hadn't released your magic, we wouldn't have gotten out of there. You did what you had to."

Maybe, but that didn't make me feel any better.

"Breathe," Mom demanded and reached out to touch me.

"Don't, you'll get hurt." I felt awful for what I'd done to Egan. "I need to calm down first." I sucked in air and held my breath for a few seconds before letting it out and repeating the action. How my clothes and the seat weren't frying was beyond me. It was as if my magic knew where to channel itself.

After several long minutes, the intensity of the power subsided. My blood didn't feel like it was boiling, and my heart rate calmed.

Donovan pulled me into his arms.

"Wait." I tensed, afraid I would hurt him again. "I need a few more minutes."

"Nope, no more." His hold tightened, and he put his

face in my hair, inhaling my scent. "You're not getting out of these arms."

I readied myself to move away. "Am I burning you?"

"No, not at all." His fingers dug into my side. "I figured when your eyes stopped glowing, this would be safe."

My eyes glowed? They'd never done that before. It had to be my fae side.

Yeah, that's why the guards stopped. He placed his forehead against mine and kissed my lips gently. *I was going insane being apart from you.*

Well, it's a good thing you didn't. Being here in his arms was the safest I'd felt in days. I breathed in his musky, rainy smell and laid my head on his chest to listen to his steady heartbeat. *There's no place I'd rather be.*

Good. He kissed the top of my head. *Because you won't be leaving here anytime soon.*

A strange popping noise sounded in my head, and a familiar fae voice filled my ears. *You broke the barrier.*

We hadn't been out of danger five minutes, and the fae had already gotten a read on me.

CHAPTER EIGHT

The best option was to be honest with Naida. "I didn't mean to. It was an accident."

"Babe ..." Donovan leaned back and squinted at me. "What are you talking about?"

"Honey." Mom turned around and patted my arm. "Are you okay?"

"You didn't hear her?" Was my mind playing tricks on me? But her voice had sounded so real.

"Who?" Donovan's forehead creased, and he glanced around the car. "I didn't hear anything."

"I didn't either." Titan turned onto the interstate, heading north on I-75. "Maybe your magic or something is messing with you."

"You were hyped up like the Energizer Bunny." Mom kept her hand on my arm. "Maybe it's your magic doing weird things to you."

"Maybe ..." But it had sounded so real and just like her voice.

Sadie, I can't hold this connection for long, Naida

hissed. *Meet me at the gas station three blocks south of the school. We need to hide you before the others are alerted.*

No, this wasn't my imagination. I pulled away from Donovan, even though I didn't want to, and removed Mom's hand. With how volatile I felt, I didn't want anything bad happening to them.

"Hey, calm down." Donovan sounded like he was talking to a frightened child. "You're okay. You're safe now."

"No, she spoke again." This made it official—I was crazy. "You had to hear her."

Concern filled Mom's eyes as she looked at my fated mate. It was like I wasn't even in the car. "Maybe she should get some rest."

My fae magic bubbled inside me again. I had to get control over my emotions since they triggered my magic. Any time I got scared, upset, or whatever, it was like a tidal wave. The only reason things hadn't gone south back at the condo was because my magic had been caged. It had taken almost losing my friends to break the dam and cause my magic to flood back inside me.

This infuriated me. Dealing with this power made me feel like a newborn. I now understood all too well how Axel and Donovan had felt not so long ago. I'd never been in control of these powers, but it hadn't been an issue. It was like my magic was on crack or something. It was stronger than it had been a week ago, and I had no clue why.

"She said to meet her at the gas station three blocks south from school." I closed my eyes and focused on calming the raging inferno inside me. "She wants to hide me before the other fae feel me again."

"Is it safe?" Titan frowned as he kept his attention on the road. "Maybe it's a trap."

For it being so early, traffic was heavy. That would work

in our favor if Tyler sent the others to run us down. We'd be harder to find.

"She helped me last time and tried to give us a head start on Brock and his shifters." I trusted her. The way she'd looked at me when we'd parted ways still unnerved me. "And she seemed to know Rook."

"What?" Mom gasped. "Why would you say that?"

"When she hid my magic, it was like she recognized it." I chewed on my bottom lip. It sounded strange to say it out loud, but I knew what I'd seen and felt.

"Then we'll go meet her and get her help." Mom nodded, the decision made.

"But ..." Titan glanced at her. "We need to get back. We don't need to invite any other potential issues right now. We have enough."

"First off, my daughter is not an issue." Mom pointed her finger at him. "And second, if this woman helped Sadie before, we're going to trust her to help again."

I didn't want to add that Naida had gone back to the fae realm after she'd left me. Maybe the fae had turned her, but my gut said no. If I informed them of that, Titan would blast past that exit without a second thought. I'd tell them when it would be too late to turn back.

"I didn't mean Sadie was a problem." He huffed. "I just meant we have Tyler and the fae hunting her down."

Donovan tensed beside me and said, "I don't see how that changes what you said."

"He's not wrong." I didn't blame him for feeling that way. Mom and he had been safely hidden without anyone looking for them until I'd walked into the picture. "Maybe I shouldn't stay with you."

"Hell no." Mom tensed and faced me. "If you leave, I'm going with you. It's that simple."

"Your whole pack will be at risk with me there." Not to mention Cassius and his nest. "Maybe I should—"

"I left you once, and I refuse to make that mistake again." Mom sucked in a breath. "Besides, this fae will fix this again. No one needs to go anywhere."

The car descended into silence, and thankfully, my magic subsided. I laid my head on Donovan's shoulder and fell fast asleep.

A WARM, calloused hand brushed my cheek, waking me. My favorite smell in the entire world surrounded me. I blinked as I took in my surroundings inside the car, and everything we'd been through sprung in my mind. It was nice waking up in Donovan's embrace again.

I lay on his lap and smiled.

I missed seeing that. He looked at me with such adoration. *Not having you with me these past few days was worse than anything I've experienced in my entire life.*

That was saying something. He'd grown up in foster care with Axel.

"We're pulling into the gas station," Titan said with displeasure. "If anything seems out of sorts, we're getting the hell out of there. Is that clear?"

I sat up and glanced behind us at the van. "Do they know what's going on?"

"Yes, I told them." Donovan nodded. "I told them to head on back to the house, but they wanted to stay close. They're afraid something might happen and want to be near."

"But I trust her." That should count for something. "She went back to the fae realm, but there was something in her eyes. She looked at me like she knew me, which was crazy."

My eyes automatically found her. She stood at the edge of the gas station closest to the trees, her teal hair reflecting the sunlight. The closer we approached, the more radiant her eyes became. They were the same shade as her hair. I was learning that most fae's hair and eyes matched, except for mine. I guessed that was another way I differed from the rest.

She stood stiff as a board next to the building, obviously uncomfortable. Her white shirt blew in the wind over her jeans.

Roxy linked with the pack. *Do you want us to get out with you?*

No. Fae didn't like other races for many reasons. So we didn't need to overwhelm her. *We don't want her to feel threatened since she's helping.*

Got it, Roxy said without enthusiasm. *But if anything odd happens, I'm coming out.*

I'd be the same way. *That's fair.*

Donovan took my hand and asked, "I get to join you though, right?"

I wanted to do this alone, but he'd already been through enough these past few days. I couldn't tell him no. "Sure, but let me do the talking, okay?"

His shoulders relaxed. "That works."

Titan pulled into the spot next to the fae, and the van pulled in beside us.

A few humans were at the gas pumps but didn't seem to pay Naida any attention.

I opened the car door. "It shouldn't take long, but don't freak out. I'll use the pack link if something goes wrong."

"Fine." Mom sighed. "If Roxy gets out, I'm joining her."

"Okay." Fae didn't like humans, and they wanted their existence kept secret like we did. "Just don't overreact." I got out of the car just as Donovan shut his door.

He walked to the front of the car and waited for me. We intertwined our fingers and made our way to Naida.

"You're here," Naida said in her soft but strong voice. "I was getting worried."

"Well, we were in Atlanta." I stopped a few feet away from her. "Those shifters caught me, and I broke out this morning."

"Oh, I thought you got away that night." Naida's face fell. "I feel bad about leaving you."

"No, there were more shifters outside the dorm, and you had no clue. There's no reason for you to feel bad about that."

"Well, you're safe now." Her eyes went to Donovan. "And who's this?"

"My mate, Donovan." I lifted our joined hands.

"Then why do I smell someone else on you?" She sniffed the air, her brows furrowed. "It's not his scent."

Donovan's jaw clenched.

"A shifter claimed me against my will." I hated that this was a point of discussion right now. "Look, the more time we waste, the likelier the fae will know I'm here. Can you help me?"

"Yes, I can." She stepped toward me and lifted her hand. "But you'll want to let go of his hand so our magic doesn't harm him."

"Okay." I released his hand. *She's going to touch me, so don't be alarmed.*

Donovan stepped closer but didn't touch me. *I'm right here if you need me.*

She touched my arm like the last time, and her magic

poured inside me. It twirled along with mine, connecting and threading together.

The farther her magic reached, the more the static electricity increased. My body grew hot like earlier today, and her magic unwound from mine.

"No," Naida whispered, and more of her magic pooled inside me.

It felt similar to mine, but it charged my own even more. My breathing became labored as the overwhelming feeling from earlier coursed through me. Right when I felt like I might lose control, my magic was moved into my center and locked up tight again.

She removed her hand from mine. "I ..." Her eyes widened. "I was barely able to do that. You better be careful. I won't be able to do it again."

It was strange. Even though the magic had been overwhelming, it felt like part of me was gone. "Thank you. I appreciate your help."

"You're welcome." She licked her lips like she wanted to say something else, but Donovan interjected.

"Let's get going." Donovan touched my arm, drawing my attention to him. "We need to get away from campus as fast as possible."

"You're right." I faced Naida. "Thank you for your help."

"Actually, I'm going with you," Naida informed us as she took a step closer to me. "I'm not sure if that barrier will hold, and I'll need to be close by to keep an eye on it."

"But ..." Her wanting to come with us surprised me. "You have classes and a life."

"It's no big deal." She pointed to a teal bag at her feet that I hadn't noticed. "I already packed my stuff."

"We're going somewhere hidden—" Donovan started.

"This is nonnegotiable." Naida lifted her chin, and her voice turned authoritative. She expected to be listened to without question and picked her bag up. "Besides, since my magic is linked with yours, I could find you on my own if I had to."

In other words, she was coming one way or another. "Okay, but you'll have more room in the van."

"That will work." Naida walked over to the van, not bothering to wait on us.

Uh ... why is mermaid girl coming over here? Axel asked uncomfortably.

Because she's coming back with us. I paused for a second. *She's riding with you all if Lillith is okay with the plan.*

Lillith is fine with it. Katherine vouched for her too. Axel sighed. *Let's get back to the mansion. I'm exhausted.*

We all got into the cars, and I filled Titan and Mom in on what was going on. Surprisingly, Mom was very receptive of the news. Titan grumbled, but soon, we were back on the road, heading home.

WE GOT BACK to the mansion around noon, but it could have been midnight considering how tired I was.

"Are you sure you don't want to stay at the pack house with us?" Mom asked one last time as I opened the backdoor.

"I'm sure." Even though we were forming a relationship, I still didn't want to stay with them. If we set that precedent, they might expect us to join Titan's pack, and I wasn't sure I was willing to give up being an alpha just yet. It felt right. "All our stuff is here, and honestly, I want to stay somewhere familiar."

"Okay." She yawned, and the circles under her eyes appeared even darker. "Come by tomorrow for a visit?"

"I will." I patted her shoulder, got out of the car, and shut the door. Once Donovan had climbed out, Titan drove away.

The door to the mansion opened, and Cassius and Dawn stepped out. They hurried to Lillith and pulled her into their arms. It was easy to see the resemblance between those three. Lillith's dark hair and eyes matched her father's, and she loved emphasizing their color with her unique gothic style. Even though her mother had dirty blonde hair and light brown eyes, she had the same sharp, angular features.

"Katherine!" Julie cried as she ran out the door with Paul on her heels. She had her light blonde hair pulled into a bun, and her stunning cinnamon eyes twinkled as she looked at her daughter. She was shorter than her daughter by a couple of inches.

Paul's dark hair shined from the sun, and his gray eyes scanned his daughter from head to toe. He was taking inventory, looking for any bruises or marks.

"I'm fine." Katherine smiled, and her brown eyes almost glowed. She flipped her long, dark brown hair over her shoulder. "I wasn't in harm's way once, despite my protests."

"Hello," Naida said awkwardly, watching the display of affection.

"Oh, Naida." Dawn walked over to her and held out a hand. "We have your room ready for you."

I should've known that Lillith or Katherine would inform their parents. It made this less awkward.

"Do you need anything from us?" Lillith yawned. "If you don't, I think our group needs to crash for a while. None of us have slept much these past few days."

These people had risked their lives to save me.

"Of course." Cassius waved us inside. "We'll get Naida settled in, and you can come down for dinner whenever you're ready. Julie went to the grocery store, and she's planning a feast for you all tonight."

"That sounds perfect." I smiled. She was the best cook.

"Let's go," Roxy said through a yawn as she grabbed my arm.

Our group went inside and headed past the large living room.

"I'm glad you're safe." Lillith smacked me lovingly in the arm. "We were worried sick about you."

"Yes, we were." Katherine hugged me. "It's nice to have you back."

"Thank you." I dragged Lillith into our embrace. "You both being there for me means the world."

"I hate to break up this moment." Donovan pulled me away from the girls. "But my mate needs sleep. How about we continue this later?"

"Sure ..." Lillith snorted. "Sleep. Is that what we're calling it?"

"If you're trying to embarrass me, it won't work." Donovan picked me up, and cradling me in his arms, he walked down the hallway to the staircase to our room.

"See you two later." Roxy giggled as she, Axel, and Egan followed close behind.

When we got upstairs and into the hallway, Roxy cleared her throat. "No rough sex, okay? We're going to actually try to get some sleep."

"Oh, we are?" Axel sounded disappointed.

"Sorry, man." Donovan put me on my feet and punched his friend. "Better luck next time."

"Tell me about it." Axel pouted as he looked at Roxy. "Not even a quickie?"

Roxy opened the door and stepped inside. "Maybe ... if you can convince me."

"Challenge accepted," Axel said as he slammed the door. Giggles erupted from their room.

Donovan rolled his eyes. "I guess those rules only apply to us."

"Yeah, this isn't uncomfortable," Egan said as he opened his door, which made me pause.

"Egan?" I stepped toward him and looked at his neck. The burns had already healed, which made me feel a little better, but not much. "I'm sorry. I didn't mean to hurt you." I gestured to his neck.

"That was nothing." He grinned at me. "A small price to pay for your safety."

"But I hurt you and almost got you shot." I felt like an asshole.

"You also saved me." He lifted an eyebrow. "I saw what you did to that bullet. I'd do it all over again if you needed me."

The dragon shifter was so much more than what the stories said. "You're one of my best friends, and I consider you family. I just want you to know that."

He touched my shoulder and smiled. "I feel the same way about you." His gaze moved to Donovan and then back to me. "Go spend time with your mate. Both of you need it." He winked at me and closed the door.

I entered the large bedroom that Donovan and I shared and turned to him. Now that we were here, I was nervous. Brock had claimed me, and I'd scared Donovan back at the condominium.

He wrapped his arms around my waist. His face lowered to mine, and he took a deep breath. A frown marred his face as he suddenly pulled back. "No, we can't do this. I still smell them on you."

My heart shattered as he confirmed my worst fear.

CHAPTER NINE

I tried to prevent him from feeling how much it hurt through our bond. "Yeah, okay." I turned and faced the bedroom, embracing the feeling that I'd finally made it back home.

The off-white walls were so comforting after being stuck in a blindingly white room. The wrought iron king-sized bed sat in the center, its blue sheets still askew from the moment we'd almost claimed each other before the fae attack.

I walked past the matching chest of drawers to the end table on my side of the bed and looked out the two large windows at the woods. My eyes burned from tears I didn't want him to see.

"Hey," he said and walked over to me. "What's wrong?"

It hurt, but this conversation was inevitable. "Nothing." The air around us smelled like sulfur, proving I'd lied.

He placed a hand on my shoulder. "Between your actions and the smell, I'm going to go out on a limb and say there's something wrong." He turned me toward him. "Why don't you tell me the truth?"

"I can't help that I smell like him." He'd said *them*, but I knew what he'd meant. He smelled Brock on me, and there wasn't much I could do about that. The trauma of that night hit me hard.

"Him?" Donovan wrinkled his nose. "Yes, you do, but that's not what I meant. You smell like that condo. Like pompous douchebag ass. I thought you might want to take a shower."

"Even a shower won't remove his scent completely." Anger raged through me. Now that I was here with Donovan and saw his disgust, it hurt worse than when Brock had bitten me.

"Don't you think I know that? Even though it infuriates me, you matter more to me." He tucked a piece of stray hair behind my ear. "I won't let him come between us, but I have to ask. Is there any way we can undo what he did?"

"Yes." There was one way. "But it's too dangerous."

"What is it?" He lowered his forehead to mine. "I need to know."

"We have to kill him." I hadn't meant for it to come out like a command—I'd only meant to answer his question—but I knew that no matter what, it was what I had to do. "But he has all those guards. It would be a death sentence to go after him."

"I don't give a damn. We have to fight them anyway." He lowered his lips to mine, only a breath away. "You are mine and will be mine in every way." His mouth crashed against mine.

At the mercy of his touch, I opened my mouth, needing more. His hands wrapped around my waist, pulling me hard against his chest.

I'm sorry you thought I meant him. He linked with me as his tongue slipped into my mouth.

I was just afraid ... The only person who had the power to hurt me beyond repair was him. The thought of him rejecting me stung me to my core.

You have nothing to fear. He lifted me up, and my legs encircled his waist. He headed to the bathroom, not missing a stroke of his tongue. *I will always want and need you. Nothing will ever change that.*

His words were a promise—one I would clutch tightly to me. It was the only thing that would get me through this.

In the bathroom, I rocked against him, causing him to stumble to the huge gray stone shower. He turned on the water and growled as he set me on the ground.

You're going to make me drop you. He grabbed the hem of my shirt and stepped back, pulling the shirt from my body. Then his hands pushed my yoga pants to the ground.

I stood there in only my bra and underwear, naked and vulnerable.

If it weren't for his desire flowing into me, I would've thought he was doing this out of pity, but he wanted me just as badly as I wanted him.

He took a step back, and his eyes grazed my body. His breathing turned ragged, and an almost purr left his mouth. "God, you're gorgeous."

Needing to feel his touch, I stepped into him. I slipped my hands under his shirt and traced the outline of his six-pack. My body warmed as he unfastened my bra and removed my panties.

Desperation filled me, and I tugged his shirt over his head and threw it on the ground. My chest touched his naked chest, heightening my desire.

Steam surrounded us, indicating that the water was warm. I unfastened his jeans and let them, along with his boxers, drop to the ground.

He cupped my breast as he stepped out of his clothes. He lifted me once more and stepped into the rain shower.

I grabbed the back of his head, bringing his lips to mine. The warm water hit my back, adding fuel to the fire growing inside me.

You are perfect, he whispered as he placed my feet back on the ground, and his hands lowered, cupping my ass. *I've been thinking about this moment ever since you cuddled against me in the car.* He pulled away from my mouth and peppered kisses down my neck, on the side Brock had claimed.

It made me love him even more, which I hadn't thought was possible. *You don't have to do that.* It had to be hard to be like this with me while smelling another man's scent.

Yes, I do. He nibbled my neck. *You need to realize what that prick did doesn't change anything between us.*

A low moan escaped me. How I wished he could bite me and override what Brock had done. But I didn't want to think about that asshole. Everything inside me wanted to be in the moment. *I love you.* I leaned my head back against the stone wall as the water slicked our bodies.

His mouth covered my nipple. *I love you too,* he rasped. His tongue went to work as his hand slipped between my legs. He began rubbing.

I reached to touch him, but he caught my arm.

He let go of my breast and shook his head. *No, I want to focus on you.*

But ... I wanted to touch him too.

Nope. His mouth went back to work on my other nipple. *It's my turn to pay attention to only you.* He increased his pace between my legs, and the friction built inside me.

"Oh, God." I panted as I came closer to the edge. "I

want you."

You'll have me, he said as he nipped, and an orgasm rocked through me.

My body convulsed as his fingers kept their steady pace. I tried moving his hand, unable to take it any longer, but he held firm.

When my body settled, he removed his hand and positioned himself between my legs.

"Finally," I groaned. Even though I'd just released, I was desperate to feel him inside me. "I need you."

As he slammed into me, I arched my back and used the sides of the shower to lift myself up so he could plunge deeper.

Him filling me made everything feel right. My wolf howled in pleasure as we reconnected with our mate. She surged inside me, making me want to bite him ... to claim him. I pushed back against her. It wasn't right for me to claim him when someone else had claimed me.

He paused and pulled back, his dark blue eyes glowing. "What's wrong?"

"What?" I shook my head, trying to come back to the moment.

"You feel like you're fighting something." He touched my cheek. "Is everything okay?"

"Yeah." I licked my lips. "I'm just struggling not to claim you." My words broke at the end.

"Why?" He turned his neck, baring it to me. "There's no reason not to."

"But—" I started, but he kissed my lips, cutting me off.

I want you to. His tongue slipped inside my mouth as he thrust again. *Please.*

That was all I needed to hear. My teeth raked against his skin, and he shuddered underneath me. I sank my teeth into his neck, and he groaned as he pumped harder inside me.

Our emotions collided as we finished together. My wolf poured into him more than ever before, cementing our bond further. Now the only missing piece was him biting me.

My breathing came out in gasps, and I dropped onto my feet.

"That was amazing," he whispered as he bent down to kiss me again.

"Yes, it was." I pulled back and looked into his gorgeous eyes. "We have time to make up for."

"I agree." He chuckled and smacked me on the ass. "Now turn around and let me take care of you."

I gladly obliged, enjoying our alone time together.

Roxy's voice popped into my head. *Are you up?*

My eyes fluttered open, and it was damn tempting to close them again. Donovan's arms were wrapped around me, holding me tight. It felt perfect.

Hellur? she insisted. *Are you ignoring me?*

She wouldn't leave me alone. *Why even ask if you're purposely trying to wake me?*

Oh, good, you're up. She was pretending like I hadn't called her out. *I figured you might be.*

We weren't until you started pestering us, Donovan growled through the bond. *Why don't you shut up so we can get back to sleep?*

Hey. She actually sounded offended. *Tell him he can't talk to me that way!*

Axel asked confusedly, *Are you talking to me or Sadie?*

Both of you should be defending my honor. She huffed. *I*

mean, come on.

I rolled over so I faced Donovan and sighed. "We'd better get up. She won't stop."

"And why is she your best friend, again?" He chuckled and kissed me.

"Yes, she is annoying." That was something I'd learned in kindergarten. "But she's loyal and trustworthy. She's always had my back and liked me for me, unlike everyone else in that godforsaken pack."

"Fine." He pulled away from me and threw off the covers. "But we'd better not be around them for too long. I still need some one-on-one time with you."

"Don't worry." I winked. "We're on the same page about that, but it would be good to talk with Naida. I'm not sure what her plans are."

I stood and stretched, my shirt inching up my belly. I was dressed in my standard comfy clothes of a tank top and yoga pants, but they were actually mine, not the ones Tyler had picked out.

Donovan quickly pulled on a pair of jeans and a shirt and opened the door. "Let's go before Roxy comes barreling upstairs and starts knocking repeatedly."

She'd done that multiple times when we hadn't moved fast enough for her.

We walked downstairs and into the huge living room. The walls were a light gray with two L-shaped leather couches set across from each other. A huge television hung over a fireplace, and it was currently turned on and playing some killing video game.

Katherine's brothers sat at the edge of the couches, playing against each other.

"Dude, what the hell is wrong with you?" Athan hissed as he jerked his head to the side, making his blond hair fall into his gray eyes. He was Katherine's older brother, and he'd been turned when he was twenty-two.

"I'm kicking your ass." Luther pumped his fist in the air. His light brown eyes were lit with excitement and contrasted with his dark hair. He was only sixteen, but he and Katherine could pass as twins. "That's what you get for being an old man. You can't keep up with the coolness of the young."

Naida stood at the back of the room, her brows furrowed as she stared at the TV. "I don't understand how you can enjoy killing your family."

"Well, it's a game." Katherine sat next to Athan. "They aren't hurting each other."

"But they are being mean to each other." Naida tilted her head. "Isn't that the same thing?"

"They're like this even without the game." Lillith snorted and punched Luther in the arm. "Aren't you, boy?"

"Hey." Luther grimaced at her. "You're going to make me mess up."

Luther was quiet and reserved unless it came to a video game. It was the only thing that brought out his competitive side—that and his older brother.

"Did you get settled in?" Maybe ignoring their theatrics would calm Naida. "I'm sorry I didn't hang around, but I hadn't slept in a while."

"I shouldn't have left you." Naida frowned. "I should've stayed and protected you."

"You said your juice was running low." I joined the group in the living room and sat next to Lillith. "I'm not sure you could've helped out very much."

She took a step in my direction. "My juice?" She reminded me of a dog when they heard loud noises. Her head tilted even more.

"Your power. You said you might not have enough to get you back to the fae realm."

"That's true." She turned and looked out the large window. "But I should've made sure you were safe before I left."

The guilt poured off her, and its signature smell of sour milk filled the room.

"There's no way you could've known." We'd known the risk of going back and that there was a chance someone from Tyler's pack would be at the school. Granted, I hadn't thought a small army would be stationed there. That was a mistake we'd never make again.

Roxy breezed into the room and bumped shoulders with Donovan as she passed.

She glanced at the fae and arched an eyebrow. "So ... what stuff do you eat? Julie is cooking and at a loss over what to make you."

"A salad and fruit will work." Naida shifted her weight to one side and glanced at me. "Why do those people want you?"

There was no point in lying. She knew where we lived and that I was part fae. "Because Tyler claims I'm his daughter."

"But you are Rook's, right?" Her words were eager, almost hopeful. "Why would he do that?"

"Because he hopes I can create the perfect shifter heir." It made me sick, thinking about it. "He raised me to think he was my actual father. He relishes the fact that he killed my father in cold blood."

The walls began to rattle as Naida's eyes glowed. Her hands clenched at her sides as her magic buzzed.

I'd brought her here, thinking she'd keep us safe, but what if I'd brought a monster instead?

CHAPTER TEN

The walls rattled hard, and a picture of Lillith's family fell, breaking the frame as it hit the ground. Pieces of glass scattered across the wood floor.

Athan dropped the controller on the couch as the TV rocked against the wall.

I needed to get Naida's focus on me. "Naida, what's wrong?" If something happened because she wanted to come for me, I couldn't live with myself. My good intentions kept creating issues.

Her eyes glowed brighter, and her hands clenched into fists. "The man who kidnapped you killed Rook?"

Did she know your father personally? Donovan asked as he ran over to me.

I don't know. I hadn't considered that she would've known him that well. She'd looked disturbed when she'd felt my magic, but I'd thought they'd been from the same section of fae or something.

Egan ran into the room. His gaze locked on the fae. "What's going on?"

Cassius, Dawn, Paul, and Julie came running into the

room right behind him with Mom and Titan following right on their heels.

"She found out who killed Sadie's father," Lillith said and glanced around the room as another picture fell.

I'd caused this, so I had to fix it. I stood and stepped toward her.

Donovan snatched my arm, tugging me back. *Don't. She's losing control.*

No, I have to do this. I removed his hand from my arm and walked over to the fae. I didn't want to worry him, but he didn't get to make these decisions for me.

I touched Naida's arm.

Mom gasped. "Sadie, don't touch her in that state. You might get hurt."

I ignored her as the static electricity of Naida's magic swirled inside me, but unlike when she'd hidden mine, all it did was caress the top of my skin. She wasn't pushing it toward me or trying to hurt me. But I could feel her pain, and she was heartbroken.

"Hey, I'm right here." I didn't know why, but they felt like the right words to say.

My touch brought her back to the present, and as she shook her head, the walls went still.

"It's just ..." A sob racked her body as her attention turned to me. "You see, we've always wanted to know what happened to him. His magic had mostly left our lands, but there was a smaller piece that remained."

Hope bloomed in my stomach. "Are you saying he's alive?"

Could I have a chance to meet my biological father after all?

"We thought it was because someone had harmed him and we needed to find him." She blew out a breath. "But we couldn't pinpoint the magic, and it was like he'd vanished."

"Then how is his magic still around?" Donovan asked as he walked over and stood next to me. "Is it hidden somewhere?"

"No. We used so many of our resources, looking for him ..." A sad smile spread across her face. "He's nowhere, but now I know why we still feel a small piece of him."

That was when it hit me. "It's my magic, but I thought it didn't activate until you'd touched me."

"That's true, but it had a faint signature. A small piece of your essence was blowing into the world." She touched my hand. "But I only realized that when I hid your magic. Each fae has their own signature magic, but the very essence, the part that creates our magic, has a family signature to it. A piece of your father's magic will always be inside you."

I still didn't understand. I had to be missing the bigger picture. "Then why didn't you find me when you looked for him?"

"The signature was so weak we couldn't locate it." A tear fell from her eye and rolled down her cheek. "We spent four years searching for him. We didn't realize he'd had a child, so looking for you had never crossed our minds."

She cared so much about Rook, and I wondered if maybe this was his fiancée. If that was the case, why would she protect me? "You just gave up on him?"

"Rook was one of the strongest fae in our realm." Naida turned her back to me and looked out the window, lost in her own thoughts and memories. "When a fae is that strong, sometimes, even in death, they leave a signature behind. That was what we thought had happened, but we had no clue how. His death has been a horrible mystery."

"I'm sorry you lost someone you cared about." No matter what, I hated to bring that kind of pain on anyone. "Maybe you can find some peace now?"

"Peace?" She laughed loudly. "I will find that once I get my vengeance."

Okay, so fae were vengeful, which wasn't shocking. Most supernaturals were.

"How come he never told me he was powerful?" Mom asked as she frowned and stared Naida down. She stepped between the couches toward me. "Isn't that something you guys would boast about?"

"Rook wasn't a typical fae." Naida flipped her hair over her shoulder and scowled at Mom. "You were there when he died." The fae blinked and appeared in front of Mom. "Then I can find a little peace by killing you."

Titan growled and jumped in front of Mom. His eyes glowed as his wolf surged forward. "Like hell you will."

"Don't tempt me to kill you both, *wolf*," she snarled and lifted her hands, ready to fight.

Things were getting bad and fast. I had to diffuse the situation. "She didn't kill him. She was a victim like I was." I rushed over to them, needing to protect Mom. I knew Naida wouldn't hurt me. I was her only connection to Rook.

Sadie ... Donovan growled, not pleased with me. He scooted closer. *Let me know if you need me.*

I'll be fine. I stepped in front of Titan and lifted my hands. "Naida, they killed Rook to hurt my mother." I gestured to the woman behind me. "She didn't want it to happen."

"It's true." Mom's voice broke. "I'm sorry. He died because of me."

"What do you mean?" Naida tensed, but she lowered her hands. "How did he die because of you?"

"Tyler wanted me as his mate." Mom retold the story that I'd learned only a few weeks ago. "He was set on it. My family didn't have much of a choice. Tyler was our alpha heir at the time, and what he said went. His dad supported his decision. I stipulated that I wanted a year or two at college before settling down. That I would be a good and obedient mate if he'd give me that."

"This Tyler sounds worse and worse by the minute." Naida crossed her arms, her displeasure clear. "Is that where you met him?"

"Yes, we had a few classes together." Mom focused on the floor. "We didn't feel like we fit in with the humans."

All supernaturals felt like that when it came to humans. You'd think the shifters could relate to them better, seeing as we were half-human, but our animal side was part of us even then. Humans could live a life of their choosing while supernaturals lived by certain rules. Growing up, I'd been jealous of humans and in some ways wished I were one. But that had changed in the last few months, after finding my friends and family and, most importantly, Donovan.

"We both had certain pressures put on us by our families." Mom rubbed her hands together. "He was being forced to marry a girl back in the fae realm, and I was being forced into a mate bond with Tyler. We forged a connection that we'd never had with anyone before."

"Did he tell you anything else?" Naida asked sharply. "Other than the fiancée that everyone wanted him to marry?"

"No." Mom's brows furrowed. "Why?"

There was something Naida wanted to keep hidden. That didn't sit well with me.

"No reason." Naida lifted her chin and commanded, "Continue."

Titan stepped beside Mom and narrowed his eyes on the fae. He rasped, "You don't get to command her."

"It's fine." Mom sighed and took Titan's hand. "She only wants answers. It's been eighteen years. I can only imagine how she feels." Mom continued with her story. "We had sex once."

A low, unhappy growl emanated from Titan.

Mates didn't like hearing about their lover's past sexual history, but to his credit, growling was all he did.

"And about an hour after that, Tyler burst into Rook's apartment and found me there." Mom rubbed her hands along her arms. "They stabbed Rook with some kind of knife and whisked me away, back to the pack. I never returned to the university after that."

"Where can I find this Tyler?" Naida asked.

"Not sure right this second, but he was in Atlanta," I jumped in, wanting her focus to move away from Mom. I had a feeling if Naida were going to attack, she would've done it by now, but I didn't want to take any chances. "But his pack is in Nashville. We need to be careful, though. Most of his pack only obey because they have to."

"Who is Rook to you?" Donovan asked, voicing the question I'd been wondering too but had been afraid to ask. "You seem pretty invested in his story, his death, and now Sadie. So what's your story?"

Egan interjected, "I'm assuming if Sadie's magic has a similar essence to yours, you must be Rook's family. It would be wise to give us a straight answer."

"It's true." Naida nodded. "For an Earth dragon, your memory is good." She faced me. "Rook was my brother."

"Wait ..." Could this be real? Was I dreaming? Had I found more of my family that might actually care for me? "You're my aunt?"

"No, that's impossible." Mom shook her head. "Rook talked about his sister, Nads."

"Nads?" Roxy burst into a peal of laughter. "Really? Nads?"

"That was his nickname for me." Naida's forehead lined with confusion. "Why is that funny?"

She's fae, Axel scolded Roxy through the bond, but he chuckled the entire time. *She probably doesn't even know what nads are.*

"Oh, that's a slang term here for men's balls," Lillith said gleefully, ecstatic that she'd stolen this opportunity from Roxy. "Can you see why it's funny?"

"Balls?" Naida's eyes widened. "What are you talking about?"

"Family jewels." Roxy waved a hand low in front of her like that clarified it.

"I don't understand." Naida looked at me for help. "Why are they talking about jewelry?"

"Nuts?" Lillith continued.

Roxy lifted a hand. "Oh, I know. Sack."

"Just stop." I bit the inside of my cheek to prevent a laugh from slipping through. It was hilarious, but I didn't want Naida to think we were making fun of her.

Cassius cleared his throat, uncomfortable with the entire conversation. "Uh, I'm going to head back into the kitchen and help finish up the meal Dawn is preparing." He turned and walked out of the room with Dawn, Paul, and Julie.

"I don't understand what's going on here." Naida ran her fingers through her hair. "Earth is a strange place." She looked at Egan. "It makes me wonder why your kind wanted to come here."

"Earth may be strange to the fae, but it has many things

that the fae world doesn't." Egan pointed at me. "And for you, it's where your niece lives."

"My niece." Naida smiled. "I like the sound of that."

Mom arched an eyebrow and addressed the uncomfortable question we all had. "Even if she's a *dirty* half-breed?" She emphasized dirty, letting it drip with sarcasm.

"Yes, her being a half-breed is not ideal." Naida paced in front of the window. "But she is family, and I will do whatever it takes to protect her. We will keep her hidden and off the fae's radar. And finding her has answered the question of what happened to Rook. Many fae will be happy about that."

"Dinner is ready," Dawn called from the kitchen.

My stomach growled at the prospect of food. My appetite had been nonexistent, so I had a lot of making up to do.

"They found some fruit." Roxy gestured to Naida. "So you should be good."

"Actually, I need to head back to the fae realm to update them on Rook." Naida's lips pressed into a line. "I won't be gone long."

"Okay." I didn't want her to go. What if she didn't come back or worse? "But you guys can't attack Tyler until we know who was involved." I wanted to add that *I* wanted to kill Tyler. He'd taken too much from me, but she wouldn't appreciate that fact.

"What do you mean 'who was involved'?" Naida's jaw tightened. "Were there more people than him?"

"Tyler had help," Mom agreed. "And someone had to help him find that knife. Does anyone know what it is, anyway?"

"I have a hunch." Naida tapped her foot. "That's another reason I need to head back." She looked at me.

"Don't worry, we won't attack yet. We will make sure we get all the facts straight because, when we take down those who killed my brother, I'll make sure each person responsible for his death dies." And she disappeared from sight, leaving the rest of us behind in awkward silence.

"Are we sure we can trust her?" Lillith asked. "She's hiding something."

"Yes, she is." Egan scanned the room as his breathing grew rapid. "Fae can't be trusted unless they're blood."

"But I am blood." She had just informed me that I was her niece. "So that counts, right?"

His frown said it all, but he bit his tongue. Instead, he said, "Let's go have something to eat."

―――――――

DINNER WAS DELICIOUS. The table was quiet with all of the revelations of the day, but it was nice having everyone I cared about around it.

Donovan's hand was on my thigh the entire night, and he'd whisper promises of what would happen when we got back to our room.

I finished my steak and leaned back in my seat.

"Now that we're all back together, maybe we should go for a run." Roxy's eyes lit up. "It's been a while. We could run under the moon and enjoy the night."

That sounded amazing. "Yeah, let's do that." My wolf had been caged up for way too long.

"You guys deserve to relax." Dawn stood and gestured to the door. "Go on out there and have fun. We'll have clean-up duty tonight."

That was all it took for my pack, Lillith, Katherine, Egan, Mom, and Titan to stand.

I smiled at the vampire. "Thank you. I'll clean up tomorrow."

"No." Donovan took my hand. "We will. I've gotta take care of my mate." He kissed my lips, and Roxy groaned.

"Ugh." Roxy waved a hand in front of her face. "I can smell the poop on your nose from all your brownnosing."

"Sometimes I wonder about you guys." Lillith chuckled as she looped her arm through mine and pulled me to the door.

Once our group was outside, my eyes adjusted to the night sky. The stars were out and twinkling with a half-moon rising.

We were making our way to the woods when a branch snapped behind a tree a few feet in front of us.

My wolf howled in alarm, and I moved forward, ready to face the threat head-on.

CHAPTER ELEVEN

My wolf howled as my fae magic pulsed, straining against the chains. Every time we got into trouble, my magic surged, and already the chains fractured. A small amount of my magic leaked through, filling my body.

At least, it wasn't the whole reservoir. I should hopefully stay hidden, and Naida could fix it when she returned.

The wind shifted, and Torak's familiar scent filled my nose. "Torak, you scared the crap out of me."

"Sorry." He stepped out from between the trees, his dark green eyes bright. His long black hair was pulled back into its standard low ponytail.

The prick wasn't sorry at all. "You would be if I hadn't caught your scent in time."

"Sis, I love you and all, but you couldn't take me down." The taller shifter smacked himself in the chest with a shit-eating grin. "But it's cute you think you could."

"I don't know if you could, son," Titan said, stepping beside me. "You didn't see her back in Atlanta. I'm pretty sure she could kick all of our asses."

"Damn straight she could." Roxy placed a hand on my shoulder. "In fact, I'd encourage you both to duel."

"A duel?" Lillith sounded amused. "What are we, in the 1800s?"

"It sounds more prestigious." Roxy dropped her hand. "I guess you did grow up in the mountains, so it would be hard for you to understand. How about ... y'all *wrastle*? Get 'er done."

Katherine and Egan stayed a few steps back, watching the whole scene like it was a comedy act.

When those two got going, there was no telling which direction the conversation would go in. "No, we aren't fighting."

Torak gave me another shit-eating grin.

There went my trying to be nice. "I'd hate to embarrass him in front of his dad and alpha."

"Oh, damn." Axel snorted. "Dude, you gotta admit she got you there."

"Yeah, yeah." He sniffed and patted his heart. "But I love her too much to embarrass her."

"Sure, hun." Mom chuckled at her stepson. "We'll go with that."

That reminded me of what I'd overheard back in the condo, and my smile fell. I turned to Titan since my question was more for him. "Hey, I need to ask you something."

Is everything okay? Donovan asked with concern through our mate bond. *You seem upset.*

I found out something about your family. I hadn't thought about it since I'd heard it, and now my nerves were on edge. I wasn't sure how he'd take the news. *And Axel's. I meant to tell you when we got here, but with everything going on, I forgot. I'm sorry, but Titan knew your parents.*

He tensed. *Then we better get answers.*

Titan's forehead crinkled as he took in my expression. "Yeah. Okay."

I refused to beat around the bush, so I bared my soul. "Why didn't you tell us that you knew Donovan's and Axel's families?"

The older alpha winced and glanced at Winter.

"What?" Axel staggered back.

Torak snapped his fingers. "I knew they smelled familiar."

He had said the same thing when he'd first met Donovan and Axel. I thought it had been an odd comment since shifters never forgot a scent, but I hadn't pushed it. I'd thought it was impossible. I should've gone with my gut.

"You aren't making this better." Titan glared at his son. "Why are you even here?"

"Because I wanted to check on Sadie. You weren't the only ones worried about her," Torak answered as disappointment flashed in his eyes.

"I asked him not to say anything," Winter interjected. "Donovan and Axel were freshly turned and struggling for control. I didn't want to make it worse."

"Don't you dare take all the blame." Titan stood protectively beside his mate. "It was a joint decision."

"So ..." Donovan focused on me. "Who are our parents?"

"Your grandfather was a pack alpha, and your grandfather," I said to Axel, "was the beta." I quickly filled them in on everything I'd learned while at the condo.

"That was how we were at the same foster care." Axel rubbed a hand down his face. "That makes sense and explains why we felt connected with no one else."

"What happened?" Donovan faced Titan. "You didn't feel the need to protect our pack?"

"That wasn't it at all." The alpha lifted a hand. "I had no clue they were going to attack. I was at another pack, trying to gain their allegiance. You've got to remember this happened when we were younger. Tyler had felt threatened by me ever since we were kids. With over one hundred members, our pack was larger than any other pack at that time. A section of the younger ones wanted to move closer to the city, so my grandfather asked my father to split the pack in two and take them there. My grandfather would still be the overarching alpha, but my dad would be the local one. That's when Tyler's grandfather sweet-talked my grandfather into letting him build that community."

"Of course." That fit Tyler perfectly. "They jumped at the chance since they felt threatened."

"Yes, they did." Titan smiled, but it wasn't warm. "He even offered us a deal. In hindsight, that should've been a warning, but that was before their end goal was clear. We thought they were cutting us a break because we were wolf shifters."

"You've got to understand," Winter interjected and took Titan's hand, standing beside her mate. "Back then, they presented themselves as involved, caring members of society. Only their packs knew how they were, but we were forbidden to speak out."

The amount of terror that family had inflicted on everyone was unjustifiable.

"She's right." Titan nodded. "There were rumors of them taking out people who got in their way, but they were unfounded at the time. Many people just assumed it probably involved other jealous supernaturals. Now we know the rumors were red flags that no one paid attention to."

Looking the other way was easier. However, going to war with your own kind wasn't something anyone should jump at, so I couldn't blame them. I bet back then, no one had had a clue what they were capable of.

"What happened?" Axel asked, eager to hear more. "I'm assuming there's more to the story."

"Unfortunately, there is." Titan sighed and looked at the sky. "Tyler's grandfather built our neighborhood. We only needed about twenty-five houses built because only the younger shifters wanted to access the modern niceties of the world while staying on the outskirts near the woods. After we moved in there, Tyler's grandfather died suspiciously."

"We believe Tyler's father was tired of waiting to take over and killed his dad," Winter said with disgust. "I may have been a young girl, but even then I knew the funeral Tyler's dad gave his father was atrocious."

"But it didn't matter." Titan shrugged. "No one thought they were a real threat, so everyone believed the lies they told and swept it under the rug. Moving into that neighborhood outside of Nashville allowed me to go to a better school. It's where I met your parents and Tyler."

"Let me guess," Egan joined in. "You all hung out with Tyler as the leader of your group."

"I was an eighth-grader at that point, and yes." Titan rolled his neck. "Tyler and the others had been together for a while, but your dads weren't huge fans of Tyler's. Well, I learned that after a short while. Tyler was cruel, even at that young of an age."

I could only imagine. He'd been born a narcissist. He believed what he did was right, almost like he was a god. "He thinks he's above everyone and everything."

Donovan stepped into me and reached for my hand. His eyes stayed glued on Titan as he said, "That had to be when he began getting jealous of you."

"Yes. Your fathers and I got close." Titan shrugged. "I didn't realize Tyler could tell, but he did. He felt excluded and blamed me for coming between them." He waved his free hand like he was swatting away the memories. "Anyway, long story short, your grandparents and my old man became close as well since the three of us hung out all the time."

"What caused them to go after their pack?" I gestured to my mate and Axel.

"It would be easy to say there was one event, but it was more complicated than that." Titan inhaled sharply. "You have to understand humans are seen as weak, so Tyler's family already looked at your pack unfavorably because your grandparents had mated with humans."

Axel pinched the bridge of his nose. "Then why did Tyler hang out with our parents?"

"Because they were half-wolf shifter and stronger than the humans at school." Titan lifted a hand. "You've got to realize it all comes down to power."

That was when a piece of the story echoed in my mind. "Donovan's and Axel's dads found human mates, didn't they?"

"Yes, they did." Titan nodded. "Tyler told them they couldn't mate with them, that it would ruin their pack, but they refused to listen. They told their mates about their world, and they accepted it."

"How could they be mates?" Katherine nibbled her bottom lip. "If they were human, that is?"

"They must have had some wolf shifter in them." Like Donovan and Axel had when we'd first met them and thought they were human. "That's the only thing that makes sense unless they weren't fated."

"That was exactly it." Titan smiled genuinely. "But it

didn't matter to Tyler since they were still mainly human. They ignored him and mated with the humans. It infuriated Tyler and his father."

Winter wrinkled her nose. "They thought they should be obeyed even though they weren't their alpha. That's when everything changed for our race."

"A few years later, Tyler and his father began taking over packs, and that was when your grandfathers aligned with my dad." Titan frowned at the memory. "Dad was strong, and I was even stronger, but I wasn't ready for that responsibility back then, or I didn't think I was."

I had a feeling this was when everything took a turn for the worse. "I take it you were attacked?"

"Yes, but it was the Hermunslie's pack first." Pain etched into Titan's face. "Donovan, your dad called me and told me random wolves were stalking his pack and they needed our help. Dad called my grandfather, who rushed down here, and ten of us went over to help your pack with the threat. But when we got there ..." He trailed off as the horror replayed in his eyes.

"Honey, you don't have to finish the story. I can," Winter said with pain.

"No." He straightened his shoulders and looked at Donovan. "The boys need to hear the truth from me." He paused to collect himself. "It was a slaughter. Not only did I lose my two best friends that day, but I also lost my chosen mate, who'd refused to stay behind, my grandfather, and my father. I fought, but more and more of Tyler's pack came in. I looked for you two, but you were gone. It was like you'd vanished, and I had to get back to my pack before Tyler attacked them."

"You took your pack back home to the mountains?" I bet making that decision had been hard.

"Yes. I didn't want any part of city life any longer." Titan shivered. "Since I retreated with my pack, Tyler left us alone. I don't know why. We built a life there, and one of his pack members would visit from time to time to make sure we weren't doing anything."

"How did you get here?" Torak asked, and I realized he must not have been there when Titan had explained it to me when we'd first arrived here.

"This was family land that no one knew about." Titan looked lovingly at Mom. "When this gorgeous, doe-eyed woman showed up in my small town, trying to hide from the man who'd taken everything from me, I relocated our entire pack to this land. We built homes that no one would have the blueprints to and made friends with our neighborhood vamps, who helped hide us."

"Huh, I never knew that." Torak tilted his head. "I figured we'd always lived here."

"You were only a few years old when this all went down." Winter patted Torak on the shoulder. "Of course, you wouldn't remember it. You grew up knowing nothing else."

Donovan squeezed my hand. "Do you have any clue who took us to the orphanage?"

"No, but I have a feeling it was someone from your parents' pack." Titan wrapped an arm around Mom, pulling her close. "Tyler's family took over that pack, but they were loyal to your parents. I bet Tyler had no clue they had children. It was just a series of unfortunate events, but they couldn't risk keeping you because you were mostly human, and it would have caused problems. They probably saved your life."

I realized how awful Tyler was, but the more I learned, the more I hated him and anyone who willingly aligned themselves with him. It took me by surprise how much I could detest a person. "And we need to save theirs in return." There was only one option, and it became clearer with each passing day. "We need to help everyone. He enjoys ruining people's lives. We can't let someone like him live."

"You're right." Titan huffed, but his body straightened. "They're only going to get more powerful and untouchable. We have to do what I was afraid to do all those years ago."

"Yes, we can't let ..." I trailed off as dizziness hit me hard. Dread sank deep inside me, and I grabbed onto Donovan's shoulders to steady myself.

I whispered the words none of us wanted to hear. "The fae are here."

CHAPTER TWELVE

"What?" Mom hissed and spun toward the woods. "Your magic is blocked."

"Yeah ... about that." I honestly hadn't thought it would amount to anything. "When Torak scared me, my magic broke the barrier a little."

"What?" Donovan tensed. "That's important information to know."

"Other things got brought up, and I thought it wasn't a big deal." Boy, had I been wrong. "Only a small trickle is escaping." It wasn't enough to make my power strong.

"Usually, it wouldn't be an issue." Egan's shoulders stiffened as he scanned the area. "But they're looking for you. They probably got a hit when you popped up earlier and then disappeared, so they jumped at the next opportunity to locate you."

Great, we had fae breathing down our necks. "We need the iron."

"I've already linked with the pack." Titan looked back at the mansion. "Should we go let them know and grab what you have here?"

"Yeah, I'll be right back," Lillith said and ran back toward her house. "Katherine, come with me so we can grab everything."

I hated to put Cassius and the rest of the nest in danger, but hell, they already were in danger just by being close by. From what I could tell, the fae weren't trying to hurt anyone on purpose except for me.

"Maybe we should help them," Roxy suggested as she glanced over her shoulder at the vampires' retreating figures.

"I don't want to risk the fae attacking their home." I'd already caused enough problems and didn't need to add more. "If you want to go, that's fine, but I'm staying here."

"No, I'll stay close in case they come." Roxy shook her head. *There's no way I'm leaving your side, especially after what happened last time.*

That's something I can agree with, Donovan said, siding with Roxy. *Seeing you being taken away with a bag over your head is something I never want to experience again.*

In some ways, their experience had been more traumatic than mine. I could only imagine what it would do to me if I had witnessed a loved one getting kidnapped while being helpless to do anything about it.

"There are a lot of them." Egan blinked, which was the only sign that the fae were affecting him. "More than last time."

With how dizzy I felt, I had to agree. If Donovan hadn't been supporting me, I'd have been on the ground.

"Do you think Naida caused this?" Axel asked. "What if she brought them here? She's been gone a while. Maybe your chains breaking slightly is just coincidental."

"No." There was no way. "She's been helping me."

"Has she, though?" Titan challenged, on board with

Axel. "She disappeared about an hour ago, and now they're here. It seems awfully suspect."

When he put it like that, it was hard to disagree. "But ..."

Babe, you don't even know her. Donovan linked only with me. *I'd hate for you to get hurt. Maybe Rook wasn't even her brother.*

Could it have all been a big manipulative countermove? Would someone be that cruel? Probably. I'd grown up with someone just like that, if not worse. *Do you think she did?*

His arm wrapped around my waist. *I don't know, but I want you to be prepared in case she did.*

I wanted to throw a fit and tell them they were all wrong. Her magic felt familiar—familial—but they had a point. Even if she was family, that didn't mean she didn't want me dead. *You're right.* I hated to agree, but I needed to be realistic.

The vampires all ran from the mansion, holding pieces of iron in their hands. Egan and I were screwed since we didn't have any gloves. Both he and I couldn't touch iron without draining our magic.

When they reached us, they handed iron to everyone except for Mom, Titan, and Torak since they lived at the pack house. That just proved we needed to keep extra iron on hand, but we hadn't thought we'd be going into battle tonight.

"Okay, we need to hurry." Titan waved his hands toward the pack homes in the woods. "We need to find my pack before the fae attack them."

"Let me go first." Even though my head still swam, I got steadier on my feet. It took a few minutes for me to find my grounding when fae appeared in our realm, but the longer they were here, the better my balance became. "I can feel their presence better than anyone else." Well, maybe other than Egan.

"I'll take the back in case they come from behind," Egan proposed and positioned himself behind the vampires.

That was the best plan we had. "That sounds good." I glanced at everyone. "Ready?"

A few people nodded, and the rest held their iron, indicating we should go.

I took off into the woods, Donovan following close behind me. I didn't pay attention to the order of our group; I just focused ahead.

Donovan linked with the pack. *Sadie, if you sense anything weird, even if you aren't sure, alert us.*

It annoyed me that he'd even say that, but I buried it down. We were all stressed, and I could feel how much he hated me leading the charge. He wanted to protect me, but he couldn't do that anymore. I was on Tyler's and the fae's most wanted list. *I will. Stay close by.*

Silence descended amongst everyone, and the trees flew by as we rushed through the woods. We moved at a decent pace but slow enough to remain silent. It wouldn't be wise to further alert the fae. If they still couldn't sense me, that would work to our advantage. They'd be struggling to find us and looking to Naida for direction since she knew where we were. Hopefully, she would lead them back to the house first, giving us time to meet up with the other pack and prepare.

The deeper we got, the less the raccoons and other night animals scurried, indicating that something they perceived as a threat was nearby.

Great. *Is it just me, or are the animals all hiding?*

Roxy's anxiety filtered through the bond. *There are definitely no animals.*

Dammit, Donovan growled. *Of course, the fae would be out here in the middle of the woods. That's how it was last time.*

Power flowed from the ground like the fae were channeling their energy in search of something ... me.

I stopped and faced the group. I placed a finger to my lips, and Egan nodded.

He felt them too.

His agreement frayed my nerves. The last time we'd fought them, it hadn't gone too horribly, but I'd faced a scary dark purple fae who hated my guts. She'd made them leave after we'd used the iron against them. The rage in her eyes still shook me to my core. She'd left, vowing to come back and finish the job. I had a feeling they were back to do just that.

I pointed at my eyes for those I couldn't speak to and linked with my pack. *Keep your eyes open. They're near.* I gestured right, hoping to avoid the fae. The power was coming from the left side of the woods. If we moved fast, we could evade them for a while.

Titan and Cassius nodded, making me feel more comfortable. They'd lead their groups, so I only needed to worry about mine.

Egan motioned for me to go, confirming he was on the same page. With those three on board, my worry eased.

I spun on my heel and hurried to the right, everyone's footsteps following behind me. It seemed like the fae countered each step I took farther into the woods. The cold, stark truth rocked me.

They'd caught my magic and were on the hunt.

They're on the way. I linked with the group and pushed myself to run faster. Any concern about being quiet left me. They were already tracking me.

Roxy's voice was full of alarm as she filled in the rest of the group. "They've located us. We have to move faster."

Our group picked up speed, and we pushed hard, trying to reach the other pack before the fae caught up.

Fae magic surrounded us, indicating they were close. It was strange because I'd never felt it like this before. I couldn't see the magic, but I felt it deep inside me. My trickle poured out in response to the surrounding magic.

"Stop!" I yelled and dug my feet into the ground. Not too far ahead, the fae were waiting on us. The magic was so strong it was palpable. "They're right ahead."

"My men are close by," Titan whispered. "We'll have backup soon."

That made me feel a little better, but there was no preventing this. They wouldn't wait much longer. I circled back so I was closer to Egan. "I think they can feel Egan and me. Maybe you should go first and catch them by surprise." I hated to suggest it, but it might be the best way to gain the upper hand.

"She's right," Egan backed me. "And we can continue right like we aren't aware of their presence and hopefully catch them off guard."

"I'll stay back with them." Donovan adjusted the long piece of iron in his hand. "That way they'll have protection for when the fae figure out our plan and find them."

"Okay." Titan stepped in front, ready to lead. "Let's go fast and hard. My pack should join us in less than two minutes."

Cassius motioned ahead. "As soon as you're a few feet ahead, we'll charge forward."

This made me sick, but I didn't have a better plan. "Okay. Let's go." I went right with Donovan and Egan only a step behind. The three of us rushed away from the others, and I prayed this plan would work.

We grew closer and closer to the fae. They were heading us off for a surprise attack. I slowed, and Egan and Donovan flanked me.

Of course they would. They epitomized protective alpha male, but I wouldn't change a thing about either one of them.

I heard a cry that didn't sound familiar, but I had to make sure. I rushed toward the source, and as I stepped through the last section of trees, my world came to a crashing stop.

So many fae were here that there was no way in hell we could win even with the iron. Naida had tricked me after all, making this even more traumatic.

"Holy shit," Egan gasped, and his shirt ripped off him as he shifted into dragon form. He was soon the size of a giant living room, and his wings flapped hard into the sky. Smoke curled from his nose as his fire lit inside him.

We need a different plan. Donovan sounded panicked. *There are too many here for me to protect you.*

Titan's pack charged into the clearing. They were all in human form, holding long iron pieces, and a few even had iron shields. We had at least fifty people fighting on our side, but the fae outnumbered us by at least twenty-five.

I watched in horror as my friends and family fought against the fae to protect me.

Egan roared in the sky, and fire erupted from his mouth, hitting several fae fighting below.

Two male fae ran in Donovan's and my direction, their hands glowing, and my mate stepped forward to protect me. I moved to fight alongside him, but a voice I'd wished to never hear again hissed from behind me.

I spun around right as Ensley, the dark purple fae woman, stepped into my line of sight and snarled, "It's about time you showed up. I hope you enjoyed your last days."

My magic swirled inside me and broke the barrier. I welcomed the rush of magic flooding me. This was the best chance I had to survive, although it was small. "This is your last warning." I tried to sound more sure than I was. Everyone was engaged in battle, and I wanted it all to end. "Go back to your world and leave us alone. I have no interest in causing problems."

"Oh, yeah, right." The woman sneered. "You kidnapped one of our own, so even if we were okay with impure blood-lines, we couldn't let that slide. You're destined to die, and it will be a pleasure to watch the life leave your body slowly."

Great, so not only would she kill me, she'd make me suffer. Just another thing to look forward to. "I didn't kidnap anyone." I embraced the static electricity coursing through my veins, and my blood boiled like it had earlier today.

This should catch her off guard. I only hoped I could control my magic. I held my hands out, and rose-pink power flowed out and slammed hard into the woman.

She flew backward and landed on her back. She jumped to her feet and glared. "Did you think that would stop me?" Ensley laughed. "Is that all you have?" Her hands glowed a sinister purple as she lifted them and smirked. "Now, it's my turn, and your shifter side won't be able to take the brunt of my magic."

"No!" Donovan yelled as he turned away from the fae he was fighting and ran toward me. The fae grabbed him and threw him hard onto the ground. The piece of iron fell out of Donovan's hold and rolled into the woods.

I needed to get to him. I turned as Ensley unleashed her

power right at me. It slammed into me, and I fell to the ground.

"Sadie!" Donovan cried, struggling to get the man off him. "I'm coming." But it was futile as he collapsed.

Her magic burned inside me. It didn't feel comforting like Naida's had. The purple fae's magic felt like acid on my own power. I stumbled to the ground, at her power's mercy. My magic tried to course through me, but it didn't do any good.

My eyes flicked back to Donovan right as the fae man lifted his hands, ready to pour his magic inside my mate.

If I didn't do something, everyone I loved would die.

CHAPTER THIRTEEN

I let fear and rage consume me. My emotions amplified my power; that was the only damn way I knew how to control it.

Enough people had been hurt or killed because of Tyler and me. Senseless killings had to stop, and there was no time like the present.

Seeing my mate crumble because of the male fae created a raging inferno like no other. I used it to fuel everything inside me. My blood began to boil and revolt against the purple magic.

"What?" Ensley said in shock. "How...?"

A wave of dizziness hit me as more fae joined us in the clearing. I couldn't pay attention to that now. I needed to save Donovan.

My mate screamed as magic shot from the fae's hands.

No, I had to do something before it was too late. Donovan couldn't last long.

"Stop!" a deep commanding voice shouted, making my ears ring. "Now!"

"King Murray," Ensley gasped, and her power dissipated from inside me.

His voice was filled with such authority that both sides paused to listen.

Despite a temporary reprieve, the king was here, which could only mean things would get much worse. I ran over to Donovan and stepped in front of him, blocking the male fae from getting to him. *Are you okay?* I asked him.

Yeah, he groaned, clearly not okay, but he was alive.

Taking in our surroundings, I saw that a few of our people were down, but the fae had paused.

"My King." Ensley stepped aside without turning her back on me. "What are you doing here?"

Feeling like we were relatively safe for the moment, I looked directly at the man wearing all white. He was taller than most of the fae around him and looked around Mom's age. His hair and eyes were a sky blue.

"The fighting ends now." King Murray turned in a slow circle, taking us in. "You all need to stand down."

"But why?" Ensley's face creased. "I don't understand. She's a half-breed. We can't allow her to live. It'll dilute the bloodline further."

"I normally would agree with you, but not this time." The king stepped forward, revealing the person standing behind him.

Naida.

She wore matching white, which made her hair and eyes seem brighter. Her concerned gaze landed on me, and her shoulders sagged in relief.

None of this made sense. Why was she with the king and wearing white like him? Did she serve him? But the other two people standing beside her wore black.

"But ..." Ensley shook her head and glanced at me again. "The law says she needs to die."

"And there is one law that trumps all," the king said as he looked at me almost tenderly. "It is punishable by death to kill anyone from the royal family."

Why would that be relevant? Unless ... but that was crazy.

"Are you saying she's your or Naida's daughter?" Ensley scoffed as the others mumbled beside her. "That's impossible. You've never been to Earth, and Naida hasn't been here long enough to conceive a child."

"That should answer your question." Naida smirked as she glared at Ensley. "Who's the only other possibility?"

"No." Ensley stumbled back. "Rook never would've done that to me."

"Apparently, he did." Naida flipped her teal hair behind her shoulder as animosity filled her words. "He did it with someone else. A shifter at that."

"Nads, that's enough." King Murray turned to Naida and gave her a stern look. "You'll only make this worse."

"Fine," Naida huffed but nodded. She closed her mouth and approached me.

"That law shouldn't protect her." Ensley gestured at me. "She's not a full royal."

"The law doesn't state only full-blooded fae are protected." King Murray straightened his shoulders, upset at being challenged. "Unless you're saying you know better than the king."

Ensley tensed, and her face turned into a deep-set scowl. "You'll encourage others to have dalliances with Earthlings."

Dalliances? Roxy snorted. *I swear they're living in the past.*

Maybe that's the last time they visited the human realm, Axel interjected. *So that's what stuck with them for the past two hundred years.*

Guys, Donovan moaned as he stood. *Let's stay on alert.*

He'd said *shut up* more nicely than I would've.

"Do you think my brother meant to create a half-breed?" King Murray lifted his chin. "No fae would ever intend for something like this to happen. It was obviously an accident."

Wow, they were asshole snobs even when they were protecting someone. The word *accident* from his lips sounded worse than any curse word I'd ever heard. If he hadn't been the only reason the fae weren't attacking us, I'd have fried his ass if just for a second.

"Then how did you not know about her?" Ensley challenged. "And we thought she kidnapped Naida. We came here to rescue her."

"Oh, please," Naida interjected before her brother had a chance. "You would have felt my arrival back in the fae realm and known I was safe."

"We thought you escaped." Ensley's jaw clenched, and her voice sounded strained. "We came here to protect our princess."

"Thank you for your loyalty." King Murray stepped in and gave Ensley a small smile. "But you're no longer needed here. Please take *my* army back home."

Ensley's body shook with unbridled rage, but she nodded. "Fine. Everyone, go back home." She turned to me before she disappeared. "This isn't over."

The king stayed along with Naida and the two men in black. They were identical twins with matching black hair and eyes. They were the first fae I'd seen that weren't colorful.

Once everyone had left, the king turned to me and stared without speaking.

To say it was awkward would have been an understatement.

Mom stepped toward King Murray and Naida. "Was Rook a prince?"

I could count on Mom to break the silence.

I sighed with relief when the king's penetrating gaze left me and went to her. It felt like he'd been looking for something inside me, and I had no idea what.

"Fae can't lie," Murray said simply like he hadn't expected to be challenged.

I wasn't one to follow expectation. "But they damn sure can manipulate, right?"

Sadie. Donovan took my hand in his. *Be careful. Just because they saved us doesn't mean they're not a threat.*

That's what I'm trying to figure out. The king clearly wasn't thrilled about my existence. *That way we'll know what to expect going forward.*

"I told you." Naida smiled as she walked over to me. "She reminds me of him. Unafraid and strong."

"You mean impulsive." Murray tsked as he followed her over to me. "And strong-willed to a fault."

"It looks like I'm not the only one with that last attribute." I stood tall, making it clear he wasn't my king. "If you dislike me so much, why come here and protect me?"

"Whether I like it or not, you're family," he said with disdain. "And Naida informed me that you know who killed my brother."

"Yes, the man who claimed to be my father did it." I didn't want to repeat the story. Naida had probably told him everything. "But I'm assuming you already knew that."

"Nads filled me in before we had to come and intervene." Murray glanced around the area, taking in the wolves and vampires around him.

The sound of flapping wings alerted me that Egan was landing.

"Holy hell." Murray's mouth dropped. "A dragon is here and fighting with you?"

Egan's huge, dark olive-green, scaley form landed several feet away. He couldn't shift back into his human form without being naked, but he stayed close, watching. Smoke trickled from his nostrils, making it evident that he was still alarmed.

Every person we'd come across had been shocked that we had a dragon on our side. "He's one of our best friends. We met him at Kortright, like Naida."

"Interesting." Murray tilted his head as he examined the dragon, but then his expression changed. "Ensley will not be happy that we interfered and publicly embarrassed her in front of her men."

Roxy walked over to me. "How did you embarrass her? You just told her to stand down."

"Remember that girl Rook was promised to?" Naida arched an eyebrow. "That was Ensley. It was her parents' desperate attempt to get her out of her family job."

Lillith crossed her arms. "Of being a bitch?"

"Well, no." Naida chuckled. "She enjoys that perk."

"Nads," Murray warned and focused back on us. "Of being an assassin and leader of the royal army."

"And your parents actually considered it?" Cassius pursed his lips. "I thought royals were above warriors."

"When you are a royal, it's hard to find an equal as your partner." Murray rubbed his fingers along his chest. "Especially when you're the ruler over an entire realm where warriors are very respected. It made sense for the future king to have someone strong like her by his side." Murray sighed. "Rook passing changed everything. Ensley remained stuck in the warrior role, and I being the spare stepped into role of becoming king. Not only does the job put more pressure on me, but my wife as well since we're expected to create an heir, which we haven't had any luck with yet."

I hadn't expected him to be that open with how he'd started out. "What do you think Ensley will do? Attack us still?" That woman looked at me with more hate than even Tyler did.

"No." Murray shook his head. "She will obey even if she doesn't like it."

I wasn't so sure about that, but disagreeing with him would start us off on the wrong foot. "How will the fae take it when they learn about me?"

"Not great." Naida frowned. "But if you help us kill Tyler, they might leave you in peace."

"Wait." Donovan stepped closer to me and winced, proving the fae had hurt him more than he let on. "I thought you said they'd obey you."

"Yes, they won't kill her, but that doesn't mean they'll be nice to her either." Murray glanced at Egan for a second again. "But they pretend she doesn't exist."

"And why should we trust you?" Mom leaned back on her heels. "You don't seem too thrilled about Sadie."

"I'm not." Murray's eyes darkened to a navy blue. "Her existence complicates things."

What an asshole. "Sorry my existence is making things hard on you." The contempt poured from me. "But it's not like I've got it easy here either."

"I know that." Murray adjusted his shirt. "But the fewer people who know about this connection, the better. I need to get back and perform damage control." He turned to Naida. "You'll stay here to figure out a battle plan, right?"

"Yes." Naida patted her brother's arm. "I'll keep you informed as we determine the next course of action."

"Good." Murray faced me again. "Even though your existence is problematic, I'm happy to see that a piece of Rook still lives on." He disappeared with the men in black following right behind.

"Well, that was pleasant." Katherine blinked. "I don't know what to think."

"Titan." One of Titan's pack members cleared his throat. "What do you need us to do?"

"The threat is gone, so you can all go back home," Titan replied even though a vein bulged in his neck. "Just be safe. If anything seems odd, let me know immediately."

The pack member bowed his head slightly, and they all made their way back to the houses.

"I promise no one else will attack." Naida surveyed the area. "Especially with me here. We're good."

First things first. "Let's head back so Egan can change."

The others nodded their agreement, and our group walked back to the mansion at a slower pace while Egan flew overhead. Donovan limped, which made me wish I'd been able to stop him from being hurt. Luckily, he was now a full-blown wolf shifter and should be healed in hours.

No one spoke as we all processed what we'd gone through. If Murray and Naida hadn't shown up when they did, we would have lost most if not all of our people. We'd gotten lucky, and I was so damn relieved that putting my trust in Naida hadn't been a mistake. For a long minute, I'd thought she'd betrayed us.

When we reached the mansion, Axel ran inside to find

Egan some clothing. The rest of us waited in the backyard underneath the still rising moon.

Naida lifted her head and closed her eyes. "Do you all have a plan for the next steps?"

Actually, I did, but no one would love the suggestion. "We need to go back to Nashville and steal all the blueprints Tyler has in his safe room."

"What?" Roxy's eyes almost bugged out of her head. "Are you serious? That sounds like a suicide mission."

"I don't like the sound of it either," Donovan said and took my hand. "But she has a point. The blueprints allow him to reign as he pleases. If he doesn't have them, it'll weaken his hold over the packs."

"Not if everyone still believes he has them." Titan frowned. "It won't do a damn thing but piss him off."

The solution was easy. "If we instead record destroying them on video and shared it online, everyone would see."

"You know, she's right." Cassius rubbed a hand across his jaw.

"But it won't be easy to get in there." Titan groaned. "What you're saying is right, but the blueprints have to be heavily protected."

Mom beamed. "Actually, I know the code to the room. I watched him enter it one night when he was sloshed after a meeting. He was so far gone he didn't even notice I was behind him."

Lillith rubbed her hands together. "Wouldn't he have changed it after you left?"

"You'd think, but he had no clue." Mom rolled her eyes. "Tyler is arrogant, and the thought of someone crossing him would never enter his mind."

"She's right." Tyler thought he was untouchable. "It's worth a shot."

Naida walked over and threw an arm around my shoulders. "And you have two fae who can take down at least twenty shifters on their own."

"When should we leave?" Roxy asked. "He's still out of town."

"Yeah, they have to do some damage control." My stomach sank at the thought of going back to my childhood home, but sometimes, we had to face our fears. "We should leave now so we can get in and out."

Lillith headed toward the mansion. "I'll get the van keys, and we can roll when Egan gets dressed."

"And Torak ..." Mom started.

He threw his hands in the air. "Oh, I know. Go get the car." He sighed. "On it." He took off running into the woods.

It was time for me to grow up and take my demons by their balls. I only hoped they wouldn't eat me alive first.

CHAPTER FOURTEEN

Normally, road trips felt like they took forever. The few times I'd traveled by car or plane with Tyler had felt like time had stood still. Granted, he would ignore me, and the only times he'd speak to me was when I'd do something he couldn't stand; like breathing too loud, chewing too loud, or my facial reactions not being ladylike. In other words, near-constant criticism.

So when we rolled into the neighboring woods and stopped at a pull-off in what had felt like minutes since leaving, my mental state hadn't improved, and I was about to face my childhood home of no laughter, no love, and self-hatred. I'd grown up feeling, if I wasn't perfect, which I never was, I didn't deserve love and it was all my fault. Even though I'd learned otherwise, being here made me feel like the little girl I used to be.

Hey. Donovan took my hand in the backseat of Titan's car. *Are you okay?*

No. My mind raced with the endless possibilities of what we'd find, increasing my anxiety. *But I will be.* The stench of a lie didn't fill the air, making me feel better. I actually believed it, which shocked me.

"Titan, you need to stay put." He wouldn't enjoy me telling him what to do. "Tyler will rush home, and we don't want your scent to give us away."

His hands clutched the steering wheel so hard his knuckles turned white. "And just leave my mate and you to go in there without me?"

My heart warmed at his words. He was concerned for me, and that softened me toward him. When we'd first met, he'd been growly and protective of my mom, but we'd started to come around to one another.

"Oh, stop." Mom smacked his arm. "We both know she's right. If Tyler even gets a whiff of where we're staying, it's all over. And we aren't going in alone. Donovan, Roxy, and Axel are coming with us, and Egan and Naida will be outside as backup."

I'm glad Tyler knows I'm alive. Donovan opened the back door and climbed out. *Otherwise, you'd have my ass back here with him.* He grabbed the two gallons of gasoline we'd brought to ensure we took down the whole room and fast. We couldn't stick around and risk getting caught.

That was true. I'd do anything to protect him just like he would for me. *I'd rather him still not know, but that's not an option.* I followed his direction and got out of the car.

Lillith walked around the van and faced me. "What's the plan?"

I scanned the group standing before me. "Roxy, Axel, Mom, Donovan, Egan, Naida, and I will go to the house. Then the wolves will go inside while Egan and Naida stand guard outside."

Katherine frowned. "What are we supposed to do?"

"Stay here." I understood they wanted to be part of the

action, but it would cause more problems. "And be ready in case we need you to come get us."

"No." Lillith shook her head. "That's not happening. You might need us."

"Your overly sweet scent will give us away before we get there." The guards always slacked off when Tyler was out of town, but a vampire's scent was hard to miss. "That's why we need you here."

She blew out a breath, not happy. "Fine, but if you all aren't back in an hour, we're coming after you."

"Fine." An hour would be plenty of time if everything went as expected. "And Mom can alert Titan if anything goes wrong or if we need you to pick us up somewhere. That's another benefit about you staying behind."

Mom chuckled. "That won't help."

The moon was descending, indicating it had to be around three in the morning. We needed to get a move on. "Let's go."

Titan grabbed Mom's hand and tugged her toward him. He kissed her lips and growled, "Be careful."

She nodded. "I will be."

I turned to Egan and Naida. "When we get close, you two need to stay a good half mile in the woods so, if anyone comes outside, they won't scent you."

Egan held a hand up. "How will we know if you need help?"

Good question. "Either Donovan or Axel will stay with you."

Donovan tensed and scowled. "Why one of us?"

I'd figured he wouldn't be happy with that suggestion. "Because Mom, Roxy, and I know the house. It makes sense for the three of us to go in because we can navigate it better and avoid the guards. One of you would be best outside."

Donovan cut his dark blue eyes at Axel and said, "Then it's not me. I just got Sadie back, and I refuse to be apart from her again. Last time we did something like this, she was captured."

"Fine." Axel shoved Donovan as he growled, "But if anything happens to Roxy, it's on you."

"Excuse you." Roxy flipped her red hair over her shoulder and narrowed her hazel eyes on her mate. "If anything happens to me, it's on me. No one else. You better get that shit through your head. I'm my own shero."

"Damn straight." Lillith gave a thumbs-up. "We don't need a man to protect us. We can do it ourselves."

"As touching as this girl-power moment is, we need to go." It was touching, but time was of the essence. "Titan, let Mom know if anything funny happens here too."

Knowing the others would follow, I made my way to the tree line.

The trees here were bare. A lot of high school kids hung out in this spot and had bonfires, or they used to. When Tyler realized what was up, he had the wolves scare them off. No one had gotten hurt, but after repeated multi-wolf sightings, the kids had been too scared to come back.

The others followed me, and soon Donovan was at my side, carrying the two gasoline canisters.

We walked in silence, and the trees grew thicker around us. The path narrowed, so I took the lead, heading straight to the house. I didn't know where I'd be without these people by my side. They'd become more than just my friends; they were family.

Animals scurried through the trees and brush. The sounds of normalcy eased some of the panic flitting through me. The woods and Roxy had been my saving grace during my time there.

I picked up the pace, and within thirty minutes, we were about half a mile from the house. Tyler's home was at the very back of the neighborhood with no houses close by. He'd said that an alpha needed privacy, but that wasn't the truth. Most alphas didn't need to hide their extracurricular activities or midnight rendezvous doing God knew what.

Not wanting to chance being heard, I pointed at Egan and Naida and then at the ground. I linked with the pack. *This is where you three need to stay. Alert us if you run into any issues.*

Axel sighed and stood next to the fae and dragon shifter. *I'm supposed to say that to you. Do you think we'll run into someone?*

No. I prayed they didn't. *But with Tyler, you never know. If something comes at you, do your best to hide or head back.*

Got it, Axel said and walked over to Roxy. He kissed her and blocked Donovan and me out from what he said to her.

They needed a moment. I turned to Donovan, not wanting to see the display of affection they were putting on. *Stay close. The guards shouldn't be on alert. Tyler would never expect us to do this, so I'm hoping we'll have the element of surprise on our side.*

Roxy's voice entered my head. *Okay, let's do this.*

I gestured forward to Mom, letting her know we were making the move.

Our smaller group headed through the woods. When the large, brown, stone house came into view, I almost stopped in my tracks ... almost. I took it as a positive sign.

I paused right before we broke through the last bit of trees. The large backyard was empty without a sign of a guard outside. I sniffed the air, and the coast was clear.

The house was three stories tall and over three thousand square feet. It wasn't as large as Tyler had wanted it, but he refused to alter it since his grandfather had built it. The blueprints were in the basement. We needed to get down there without alerting anyone. It was completely underground, and the only way to get to it was through the main house.

I pulled the house keys from my pocket, wanting to make sure I didn't accidentally jingle them when we got to the house. I clutched the keys in my palm and held the key to the backdoor firmly between my thumb and pointer finger.

It was now or never. *Let's go. Stay right behind me.* I linked with my pack and took off running straight down the middle of the yard. If you went left or right, it would set off strategically placed motion sensor lights. One night, when he'd been overly drunk and a little nicer, Tyler had explained that when people broke into houses, they always hung close to a side. They would never consider running right through the middle of a yard and heading straight in, so he'd placed the cameras on an angle.

That night had been hell. He'd gotten talkative drunk, but the few things I'd learned had made it worth it.

At wide double glass doors that led into a large open kitchen, I paused and didn't see anything alarming. The two young guys who were in charge usually napped around this time.

Slowly, I put the key into the lock and waited. When nothing moved, I turned it and opened the door. I tiptoed onto the gray tile floor and surveyed the room.

The pristine white cabinets looked the same as the day I'd left, and the island held the same stack of papers. Tyler hadn't been here much since I'd left, which wasn't shocking. I turned and found the other three right behind me.

I crept out of the kitchen and into the hallway. The door that led downstairs was right smack in the middle. If we could get downstairs, we'd be out of harm's way for a little while.

A loud snore sounded from the living room. Luckily, we didn't need to go that far. I was damn glad the guys hadn't changed their routines. The dark gray, wooden floors were harder to navigate. They were older and had several creaky spots. *Make sure you follow where I step.* I hated that I couldn't talk to Mom, but hopefully, she'd follow suit.

At the door, I turned the knob and sucked in a breath as I opened it. This door was known to squeak from time to time, so I moved it at granny speed.

Donovan dodged the door, which threw him off balance since he was carrying the two canisters, and stepped to the left, causing a loud squeak.

My heart stopped beating as the snoring paused.

I didn't move an inch as I waited to see if either guy would get up to investigate the sound. It was the longest minute of my entire life. When the snoring resumed, I almost cried in relief.

I waited for a few more snores before moving again. My feet hit the first step, and I descended as fast as possible while remaining silent.

The downstairs was like any standard basement with cement floors and boxes in the corner. I turned left and headed to the large steel door that went into the room that housed all the blueprints.

At the door, Mom stepped up to the keypad. She punched in several numbers.

I only hoped she'd remembered the code correctly. I hated to think we'd come all this way and risked so much just to leave empty-handed.

Donovan set a canister down and took my hand. *It's going to be okay.*

I wished his words could ease my anxiety, but only getting out of here could do that. If we got caught, it would be very bad.

A click of the lock allowed my body to relax some. I hadn't realized how worried I'd been that Mom wouldn't come through.

She opened the door, and Roxy linked with Donovan and me. *Holy shit. That's crazy.*

Inside the room were rows and rows of blueprints. They fell over the bins against both walls, and the large table in the center was covered. There was no telling how many were in here. The room alone was half the width of the entire house.

Mom hurried back to us and took one of the canisters.

I gestured to Mom to wait and rushed inside. I pulled my cell phone from my pocket and recorded the room. I circled the room and went to the middle table where I pulled out several blueprints to show the contents they held. We needed substantiated proof that we were burning the real documents.

When I was done, I waved them in. Mom rushed in and took the right side.

Guess I'll work on the left side. Donovan splashed the gas over everything. *It's going to smell and fast.*

Roxy stuck her head inside and glanced around. *You weren't kidding when you said the whole room is steel. This is insane.*

I'd only seen the room once, and it had blown my mind too. The amount of power these papers gave Tyler and his family didn't make sense.

Donovan and Mom worked thoroughly, making sure

each section got soaked in gasoline. The plan was to light the room and shut the door, containing the fire inside. That would allow us to get in and out undetected while the room's contents burned to ash.

Do we need to do anything? Roxy asked from beside me. *I feel kind of helpless.*

No, I think we're good. Maybe we could've left her behind. However, I hated doing that. She wanted to be part of this as much as I did. She had suffered at the hands of Tyler because of me. *We just wait.*

At least, I get to do this. Roxy removed the matches from her pocket. *This just adds a layer of epicness to it all.*

You basically stole it from Donovan at the gas station. The memory made me smile. Roxy had insisted that it made sense for her to start the fire due to her red hair. He'd been about to argue until I'd stepped in. *So make sure you make it work.*

She waved a hand at me. *Girl, I was born for this.*

There was no question there.

Donovan linked as he and Mom walked out of the room. *We're done. Go for it, Roxy.*

She winked at me as she lit the match and tossed it inside the room, right on top of the table that Donovan had just doused. It erupted in flames, which slowly overtook the entire room. I began recording again, revealing the room on fire. Smoke blew out and into our lungs.

Shut the door! I desperately yelled through our link. I stopped recording and fell to the ground, coughing. Donovan ran and slammed the door shut as Mom began hacking too. For whatever reason, I'd thought the door would keep the smoke inside, but I'd been wrong. It poured out of the cracks around the door.

We've got to go! Roxy exclaimed as a coughing fit hit her too. *Now.*

Smoke floated upstairs and into the hallway. It was only a matter of time before the fire alarm went off.

Shit, this had been a horrible idea.

The four of us climbed the stairs as we hacked out our lungs. Right before we reached the top, the fire alarm sounded.

We weren't getting out of here without a fight.

CHAPTER FIFTEEN

"Dude ..." a guard said. "The fire alarm is going off."

"No shit, Sherlock," the other grumbled.

We need to run. I stepped into the hallway as the floor shook. It vibrated so hard I could barely stand on my two legs, and my teeth chattered. *What's going on?*

Donovan joined me in the hallway and grabbed me by the waist to steady me. *Holy shit. The steel is weakening from the fire. I thought it'd be reinforced.*

Mom pulled Roxy off the stairs right before the railing collapsed. Mom yelled, "Move!"

Her words startled me into action. We couldn't just stand there like dummies. We'd get caught or worse—hurt.

I rushed toward the kitchen, realizing the magnitude of the situation. I'd never imagined something like this would happen, but it was too late to alter our plan. We had to get the hell out of here.

"Did you hear that?" The guard sounded panicked. "Someone's still in the house."

The four of us ran fast and hard through the door.

Somehow, we didn't fall, but my legs still shook even though we were on solid ground.

I glanced over my shoulder as the two guards came barreling toward us. Their eyes widened as the wooden floor cracked beneath their feet.

"They're trailing us," I said out loud so Mom could hear. Leading the group back to the woods, I didn't bother staying in the center. It didn't matter. Those two guys had already alerted God knew how many shifters about what had happened.

The lights flashed on as we raced to the woods, but several dark figures chased after us, closing in from both sides of the house. The wolves were here. The fire alarms were just as loud out here as inside, but the wolves were the bigger threat.

I linked with Axel. *We're being chased. Be ready to run.* They would hear us coming, but it was best to prepare them.

Right. Axel linked back with me. *I'll tell the other two.*

There are at least six wolves chasing after us. Probably more, but I didn't dare waste any time looking back again.

Got it, Axel replied. *We won't run off until we know you guys are okay.*

Hopefully, it wouldn't come to that, but four of them were in their wolf forms.

It was like Axel had prophesied what would happen because Roxy linked with the three of us. *They're breathing down my neck.*

That made the decision easy. I spun around and realized that Roxy wasn't being dramatic. They were on her. *We have to fight.* There was no other choice. The woods were just a few feet ahead.

I had to do something. I refused to allow Roxy to get

hurt on my watch. I ran to the side, and Donovan and Mom stopped too. I should've known they wouldn't let me do this alone.

Donovan stood in front of me and growled, *What are you doing?*

I snapped, *Protecting Roxy. She's at the very back and almost got attacked.* He would've done the same thing if he'd realized.

A black wolf lunged at Donovan with his teeth bared, bringing my point home. Donovan snarled as he stood his ground.

What the hell was he thinking? He needed to move out of the way.

"No!" I cried as the magic inside me swirled. I lifted my hand and shot the wolf in the chest with a quick burst. Not enough to hurt him but enough to startle him. "Stop it."

A guard from the house stopped in his tracks. "Sadie?"

I stepped in front of the group to get their focus on me. "Yeah, it's me." I'd wanted to get in and out without anyone knowing it was us, but that plan had obviously not come to fruition. I hoped that some of them wouldn't want to attack us.

"I thought I smelled you." The shorter one named Joe frowned and shook his head. "But I thought I was imagining it with the smoke. How the hell did you shock him?"

"Look, it's a long story." The less they knew, the safer they'd be. I had to ask them for a favor even though there was no way it would happen. "Just let us go. We aren't here to hurt anyone." I looked each one of my former pack mates in their eyes.

The taller guard frowned. "You know we can't do that, especially after what you just did to your house. I'm sorry."

And there it was. "I am too." I couldn't blame them. If

Tyler found out, and I was sure one of these other pack assholes would rat them out, they'd all be punished, including their families.

This brief pause at least gave us time to prepare and for my magic to ramp up. Ideally, I'd have liked for Egan and Naida to stay hidden as our secret weapons for as long as possible. "I guess we have no other choice but to fight." If they realized I wasn't all wolf, that would loosen some of Tyler's hold on them.

"Look." The taller guard raised a hand. "I'm sorry, but we have to do this. Even though you're a girl, I'll take you down like a man." I could smell the lie rolling off him. He wanted me to make it hard.

"Did he just ..." Roxy blew her hair out of her face. "I'm so damn tired of these sexist assholes." She lifted her hand, palm up, and pulled her fingers back and forth. "Bring it, ape. I'll make you cry and call out for your momma."

Clearly, Donovan agreed because he moved in front of us, ready to take on the wolves closest to us.

Before I could intervene, the same damn wolf lunged at him again, not having learned his lesson.

This time, Donovan called for his shift and rolled out of the way.

"Just come over to us, Sadie." Joe gestured to me. "We don't want to hurt you. I've reached out to Tyler, and he knows you're here. He wants you to go to a pack home and wait for him."

Of course he did. "I can't do that." They all knew why. It wasn't a secret how cruel he was to me. Tyler thought he kept his disdain secret, but even those who weren't close to him could see it. Hell, even Mike and Brock knew, but they needed me to unite their two sick, disgusting families.

The taller one who enjoyed inflicting pain on others smirked. "If you don't come, I'll come for you."

Donovan appeared beside me in his black wolf form and growled at the sexual innuendo.

Don't worry about me. The other dark wolf that had attacked him was back on his paws, and a second gray wolf moved in as well. *Those two wolves are going to pounce. I've got these human assholes.*

Okay. Donovan turned his attention to his immediate threat. *But if you need me, let me know.*

Same goes for you. It meant so much that we treated each other as equals now. He still wanted to protect me, but he'd left me to defend myself, which spoke volumes. He trusted me just like I trusted him to protect himself. *Now go. They're about to attack.*

I checked on Mom and Roxy. Mom was handling herself against a wolf, and the light brown wolf attacking Roxy wasn't being vicious, which I could tell was more for show. I realized it was her ex-boyfriend. She'd broken up with him over a year ago. He'd still been in love with her when we'd left for Kortright months ago.

"This is your last chance." The taller one cackled. "Otherwise, I won't be so nice."

"Do what you have to." The fae magic churned inside me, and I welcomed it. My wolf was restless, but I needed to stay in this form to communicate with Mom. "But I won't play nice either."

"Good, but I warned you," the taller one said and lunged at me.

He grabbed my arm, and I punched him in the face with my free hand. His head jerked back, and blood trickled from his nose. He stumbled but regained his footing quickly.

His dark, hate-filled eyes landed on me. "You got lucky."

"Sure." Goading him would make him react irrationally. "We can go with that." I raised my fists, ready to fight.

"Come on, man." The shorter guard cringed. "Stop trying to hurt her. Bring her in."

"Her father wants to teach her a lesson." The taller guard spat on the ground and wiped the blood from his nose with the back of his hand. "So I'm doing what he asked."

He charged at me, and I forced myself to stay put to see what he'd do. My magic charged me, but I tapped into my wolf instead. I needed her until I was ready to blast everyone on their asses.

His gaze flicked to my waist, which told me he planned to steamroll me. I forced myself not to react until he was only inches from me. I then spun to the side, out of his way, and he fell onto his knees hard.

This needed to end before more wolves arrived. We were playing a dangerous game. I tapped into my magic, letting my anger ignite it, and placed my hand on the arm the guy was using to brace himself.

He yelled and flinched away. "What the hell are you?" he screamed.

"I'm part fae." I let the hatred fill my face and stared everyone down. I needed them to believe I was more powerful than I was. I needed them to tell Tyler that they knew I wasn't just a wolf, which would create doubt about whether I was his daughter or not. "And Tyler isn't my father."

More wolves ran in our direction. Anxiety mixed with my anger, exploding my fae side as my blood turned hot.

I had to do something before more people got hurt.

I dug deep inside and closed my eyes. Instead of letting my emotions fuel my magic, I connected with it. I hoped, without allowing my emotions to interact with my magic, it wouldn't become as dangerous and unpredictable. There had to be a better way.

My magic responded to the connection like it had been yearning for it. My anger vanished as the magic replaced the emotion, linking me to the earth. I could feel the ground's heartbeat like it was in sync with mine.

I pulled from the ground and raised my hand. I didn't want to hurt them, just stop them. I still cared for them, and they were only trying to survive. I pushed my magic toward them, blanketing the six of them in it. I cupped my hand and created a force field around them, holding them back.

The taller guard charged into the wall and fell backward, landing on his ass hard. "How did you do that?" He got up, lunged at us again, and bounced off the force field like it was a brick wall.

Joe's mouth dropped. "She trapped us in some kind of cage. Look, there are pink sparkles around us."

Girl. Roxy linked to me. *You fucking trapped them.*

Yes. Even though I currently controlled my magic, I wasn't sure how long I could hold it.

Donovan took my free hand and tugged me, saying, *Let's go before the others catch up.*

The fact that my blood wasn't boiling and Donovan could touch me made me realize I had found the first step in controlling my magic. But now wasn't the time to celebrate.

"Run." I took off into the woods, knowing we had a chance to get back to the cars before the other wolves caught up. We had a decent head start on them.

We breathed rapidly as we pushed ourselves to get the hell away from the others. They were in wolf form, but we didn't run that much slower in human form.

Axel's voice popped into my mind. *Is that you? The wind is blowing downhill.*

Yes, Roxy gasped. *It's us. Get ready to run. Several wolves are chasing us.*

They came into view, and Naida turned and ran to the car.

Egan needed to move too. Axel would insist on being in the back with Roxy.

I said, "Go."

The dragon frowned but followed my instructions, which shocked me. He'd always been considerate, but he wasn't the type to take orders from others. At least, that was the vibe I'd always gotten from him, but we were such good friends and always on the same page that it had never been an issue.

We passed Axel, who now ran behind Roxy. Even though he and I had gotten off to a rough start, I had to admit he treated my best friend like gold. Maybe one day, we'd all get a chance to hang out and get to know each other outside near-constant threats of violence.

The wolves' pounding paws sounded like a war call, like the sound of marching soldiers chasing down their enemies, which sucked. They'd been my pack longer than my enemy, but they had no issue hurting me. It broke me all over again.

But what could I expect from an alpha who treated his own pack like shit?

Mom's voice was barely a whisper as she said, "The cars are running and waiting on us."

If it hadn't been for my wolf hearing, I wouldn't have caught a word. That was how damn fast we were running. We still had a mile left, and the wolves were gaining on us faster than I'd expected.

Shit, Axel groaned. *They're only five hundred feet behind me.*

We had to make it, but if it came down to a battle, at least, we were evenly matched. We'd stayed at the house too long, but I'd hoped they would let us go.

With every ten steps, they got one step closer. I was running on fumes since the smoke still hurt my lungs. When I thought we couldn't sustain a large enough lead, the trees thinned, and I spotted both cars pulled up by the road with the doors open.

All we had to do was get in there. *Push!* I yelled through the bond, feeling like an exercise instructor. *We're almost there.*

The next two minutes went by fast. I wasn't sure if my heart or legs were moving faster. Egan and Naida got into the van and climbed into the backseat while Mom, Donovan, and I split from Roxy and Axel and headed to the car.

A howl echoed from behind us. I waved Donovan in first; since he was in wolf form, he couldn't shut the door.

He jumped in and skidded across, scratching up the cloth seats.

I didn't hesitate to climb in behind him as Mom slammed Donovan's door shut and then her own.

A wolf bulldozed into my door, and the car tipped to one side.

I wasn't sure we'd make it out of this after all.

CHAPTER SIXTEEN

The car crashed back down on all four wheels as the rest of the wolves descended on us. I'd hoped to get the hell out of here, but with each second, it was getting less and less likely, unless we did something drastic.

Roxy linked with the pack. *Are you guys okay?*

Yeah. At least, we were for now. *Are you all?*

They're focused more on you than on us. Axel sounded concerned. *What should we do? Should we let Egan and Naida attack?*

No. I had a plan. *The more Naida uses her magic, the weaker she becomes. If I can't get us out of this, then we'll deploy her.*

Donovan jumped into the seat and glanced outside. *What are you going to do?*

It was a lot, but I had a plan. *I'll hold them off.* I connected with my magic and glanced around. I wasn't sure I was strong enough to create a force field for this many wolves. The only thing I could do was use my powers to get them to back away.

I pushed my power toward my hands, and I lifted my

hand, palm facing the wolves. I hoped the power would go through glass. If I rolled down the window, they might jump in.

The wolf that had rammed us crouched, ready to attack again. Right as his body uncoiled. I locked eyes on him and pushed the magic out. Thankfully, the power went through the glass and landed right at his paws.

He started and stared at the rose-pink stream of magic coming from my hands.

That's right, bitch. It's all me.

Another wolf charged at us, desperate to stop us.

I shot magic at him and hit him in the chest. He flew back a few feet before crumpling to the ground. Everyone paused as Titan squealed the wheels, lurching the car forward.

The van's wheels spun, kicking up dirt and gravel. Horror overcame me, but I was still connected to my power, preventing it from going insane.

Titan took the corner, and right when I was about to lose sight of them, I linked with the pack. Before I could say anything, a wolf ran straight at them. They narrowly dodged the wolf and skidded onto the road behind us.

This whole nightmare had been too close a call, but we'd actually accomplished what we'd come here to do even if it hadn't gone quite as planned. *Are you okay back there?*

Roxy answered, *Yes, we're still breathing if that counts as okay.*

I felt responsible. *I should've known about the steel room.*

She chuckled. *Girl, that might be the most fun I've ever had. Getting one over on Tyler made it all worth it. I wish I could see his face when he gets there and sees what happened.*

Maybe, Donovan growled through the bond and next to me. *But he'll definitely know who did it. I'd hoped we'd fly under the radar some.*

He would have known either way. I hated to be the bearer of bad news. *Only someone close to him could've gotten into his safe. He doesn't access it with anyone around. He definitely would've known who it was.*

"Dammit." Titan smacked the steering wheel and glanced in the rearview mirror. "The seats are torn to shreds."

"Honey." Mom took the alpha's hand. "Would you rather he have gotten captured or killed?"

She told things how they were, even when no one wanted to hear it, and that inspired me. All my life, I'd been around people with fake smiles and who talked shit behind my back. To be surrounded by people who told the truth and, hell, could handle hearing it from time to time felt right. This was what a normal and healthy relationship sounded like even when the truth hurt to hear.

"Maybe ..." He groaned and glanced over his shoulder. "Fine. You have a point, but no more claw marks on the seat. Sit down and behave. Not another scratch or tear on my baby." He patted the dashboard.

Uh ... Donovan looked at me. *Did he just talk to me like I was a dog?*

I didn't know if the situation was that funny or if the relief of getting away was catching up to me, but I broke out in laughter. *Yes, he did.*

Donovan cocked his head, making him look even more like a dog.

My sides cramped up, and tears burned my eyes. This was much-needed stress relief. I petted his head and pulled his front half onto my lap. *Just stay put. When we stop, you can shift back.*

Mom turned in her seat and pursed her lips. "Are you okay back there?"

"Yeah." I didn't mean to concern anyone with my hysterical laughter. "Just exhausted." With Donovan's head resting in my lap, I leaned my head against the window. "I might take a nap."

She smiled tenderly. "Why don't you do that? It's been a rough day with nonstop action."

Damn, she was right. I glanced at the clock on the dashboard. It was five a.m. It was insane to think that just twenty-four hours ago, I'd escaped the condo in Atlanta. So much had happened since then, and I'd only had about six hours of sleep back at the mansion.

The car became silent as the engine purred, heading back to the Smokies. My eyes grew heavier, and soon, they closed.

OUR GROUP WALKED BACK into the mansion around two in the afternoon. I was still groggy from waking up only moments ago. Donovan ran off toward our room so he could shift back into human form and grab some clothes.

We'd brought a change of clothes, but he'd slept the entire way back here.

Athan entered the kitchen, where we stood around the island, with a laptop in his hand. "I heard the night was a success." He placed the laptop on the counter and held out his hand to me. "That it was an enlightening endeavor."

"Oh, God." Katherine rocked on her heels. "He's trying to be punny."

"I'd love to hear how it went." Athan shrugged and smirked. "Please, fire away."

Roxy snorted. "I heard Lillith call and fill you all in."

Paul entered the room, his eyes twinkling. "I do have a burning question. Did you get the video we need to upload?"

It hurt that I'd grown up without all this cheesiness, but at least, I got to be part of it now. "Right here." I placed my cell phone on the island and slid it over to Athan. "I have one before and one after."

Luther joined us and walked on Athan's other side. "Make sure you still have the encryption software on. We need to make sure our IP address stays hidden so they can't locate us."

"I just double-checked." Luther grabbed my phone and sent the videos to his computer. "All we need to do is upload it to the central supernatural hub."

There was a site that all supernatural races kept tabs on. It was governed by a supernatural host that checked all the posts periodically. As long as we got enough shares, it wouldn't matter when they took it down.

Mom yawned as she watched Athan type on the computer. "Is there anything we need to do?"

Luther shook his head. "Nope. It's uploading to the main websites right now, and it shouldn't take long. Afterward, we're going to put it on some of the smaller websites to increase the visibility before it's taken down."

"Yeah," Titan said and took Mom's hand. "Tyler will take them all down as soon as possible."

Lillith sighed. "Maybe. When everything hits the fan, some will revolt."

"I hope so," Paul agreed.

Mom stepped toward the front door. "If we aren't needed, we'll head home and get some shut-eye."

Egan stretched his arms over his head. "That sounds like an excellent idea. I'm exhausted even though I didn't do any fighting."

"It's been a long day and a half." Even though I'd napped, it didn't feel like it. "Lillith, Naida's in the bedroom to the left, next to Roxy and Axel, right?"

"You want to put Naida through that?" Lillith chuckled. "Hearing those two."

"Oh, please." Roxy scoffed. "They're worse than we are. Tell them, Egan."

"Whoa." Egan lifted a hand, his face red. "Uh ..."

Kill me now. I'd thought we'd been quiet—mostly. "You know what, I'm tired." I grabbed Naida's hand and tugged her to the staircase. "Let me show you to my room." I didn't have Donovan here to help defuse the situation, which meant Roxy would only push it harder.

"What's wrong, Sadie?" Roxy called after me. "Are you embarrassed by something?"

"Obviously." Lillith snorted loudly. "Do you see how fast she's running? But let's be real; is it good if you can stay quiet?"

Roxy clucked her tongue. "See, the louder you are, the better it is."

Egan cleared his throat. "I'm pretty sure it doesn't work that way. I think they need help getting Naida situated." His loud footsteps hurried down the hallway, catching up with us.

"Thank you, Katherine, for not interjecting and sparing me the years of therapy I'd need to unhear my baby girl speak that way." Paul sounded relieved.

"You do realize she's not a virgin," Luther added. "I walked in on her—"

Katherine gasped. "Stop. Right now."

Thankfully, the three of us were heading up the stairs, getting away from the epic awkwardness going on back there.

Upstairs, Naida paused and looked at me. "Is it normal for people to be embarrassed and not open about their sex life?"

Her question caught me off guard. "I don't usually talk about it." That was a private matter between Donovan and me. No one else.

"I'm like her." Egan gestured at me. "Some things are better left unsaid."

"Interesting." She bobbed her head from side to side. "I didn't realize Earth people were such prudes. Well, Roxy and Lillith aren't, but I guess there is an exception to the rule." She touched my hand. "But they are wrong. Being loud doesn't equate to amazing sex. Sometimes, the more silent ones can do the best kind of damage."

And I thought this couldn't get worse.

Egan cringed. "Okay, here's my stop." He pointed to his door. "I'll see you later after we all get some rest." He essentially opened the door and ran inside.

Traitor. "Okay, the second door on the left is your room." Changing the topic was a damn good thing. "Do you need anything? A change of clothes, maybe?"

"I'll get some later. Right now, I want some rest too."

"Sleep well." I opened my door, slipped inside, and ran into a huge brick wall—or rather Donovan's chest. "Ow."

"Hey." His arms wrapped around my waist. "I was just coming downstairs to see what's going on."

"Everyone is taking a nap." I left out the part about our

sex life discussion. "Which sounds like heaven." I kissed him.

"Hmm," he groaned and deepened our kiss. *Are you sure you need a nap right this second?* His fingertips slipped under my shirt, brushing my skin.

My body warmed at his suggestion. Even after my embarrassment, it didn't dampen my need for him. *Maybe not,* I teased. *I could stay up for a little while longer.*

He tugged my shirt off my body in a flash. His lips connected with mine again. *Good.*

Whoa. He acted as though he needed me desperately. *What's wrong?*

I just want you. He kissed down my face to my neck. *It feels like it's been forever.*

His eagerness had me primed and ready. My hand slipped inside his jeans and boxers, and I stroked him.

Dammit, he growled in my head. He turned so he was stepping backward toward the bed. *I need you now.*

Normally, we went slower, but the idea of a quickie sounded amazing. I shoved him, and he landed on his back on the bed, and I removed his pants and boxers in one fell swoop. I grasped his shirt, ripped it off him, and tossed it to the ground.

He chuckled sexily. *Looks like I'm not the only eager one.*

I took him in, enjoying every square inch of him.

My turn. His words were a promise as he sat up and tugged my pants and panties down.

I stepped out of them as he unfastened my bra and removed the straps from my arms. He tugged my waist, pulling me back down on his hardened manhood.

My lips found his, and I slid my tongue into his mouth. I straddled his lap, taking him deep inside me in one thrust.

As I moved on top of him, he lowered his head to my breast, slipping a nipple inside his mouth. His tongue rolled over it, and his teeth raked against me before moving to the other one, causing me to move faster and harder on him.

A low moan escaped, and I didn't give a flying fuck if Egan heard. This connection between Donovan and me was the only thing that mattered. I shoved against his chest so he lay flat on the bed, and he palmed my ass to hold me steady as he scooted to the middle of the mattress.

When we got settled, I sat further on him, allowing him to hit me deeper. His fingers dug into my ass, making my body even more slippery against him.

Dear God, he groaned and bucked underneath me. *You feel so damn good.*

So did he, but I didn't have it in me to link with him to reply. I closed my eyes, enjoying the feel of his body against mine and him inside me. The bed creaked under us, but we were in the frenzy of the moment. I took him faster and deeper inside, bringing me close to the edge.

I pushed all of my feelings of love and need toward him. Now that I'd claimed him, I wanted him to feel everything I felt.

I'm about to lose it, he moaned. *Slow down if you aren't close.*

Instead, I quickened the pace. The headboard banged against the wall as our bodies convulsed with pleasure. He grunted as he finished inside me.

Holy shit. He caught me around the waist and pulled me next to him. *Now I'm ready for a nap.*

I cuddled into the crook of his arm as I breathed in his sweaty scent. It smelled even more delectable. With each passing day, our bond grew stronger. Without a doubt, no one could ever come between us, no matter what they tried to do.

He kissed my forehead, and we soon drifted off to sleep.

WHEN I OPENED MY EYES, the sun was still shining into the room. I wasn't sure how long I'd slept, but it felt longer than a few hours.

Sadie? Roxy connected with me. *Are you finally up?*

Huh? I blinked, trying to become more alert. *Yeah.*

Get down here quick. Roxy sounded funny. *You'll want to see this.*

My heart hammered. What had happened now?

CHAPTER SEVENTEEN

"D onovan." I shook him gently, trying to wake him.

"Hmm ..." he murmured and pulled me tighter against his chest. His low snoring started again.

Okay, gentle wasn't working. "Hey." I squirmed out of his hold and smacked his arm. "Roxy said something is going on."

"What?" He blinked his eyes opened. "What's going on?"

"No clue." I stood and wiped the sleep from my eyes. "She said there's something we needed to see."

"Okay." He climbed to his feet and picked up his black shirt off the floor.

I tried not to check out his package through his gray sweatpants or his abs as they contracted as he put on the shirt. The key word was *try*. My mate was so damn hot.

"If you keep looking at me like that, I won't give a damn if something is going on." He pulled me against his chest. "I'll devour you before we go downstairs."

Where the hell are you? Roxy linked with the pack. *Get down here now or I'm coming upstairs.*

"As promising as that sounds ..." I kissed him and turned toward the door. "... we better get going and hopefully get on top of a threat for once."

"Fine," he said begrudgingly. "Let's go and be responsible." He took my hand, opened the door, and pulled me through it.

We entered the kitchen and found everyone there, including Mom and Titan. Pancakes and bacon sat in the middle of the island, and the scent was strong. Breakfast must have just finished being cooked.

Everyone crowded around Athan and his laptop at the main kitchen table.

Their expressions varied from shock to intrigue—not horror. That calmed me down somewhat.

"Sadie!" Roxy exclaimed and waved me over. "Look!" She pointed at the laptop.

Donovan and I joined everyone at the end of the table, and Athan turned his computer toward us.

I couldn't believe my eyes.

Our video had been shared over two hundred thousand times. The original post showed as rejected, but the damage had been done. There was no turning back.

Athan flipped over to another tab of a wolf pack website where the post of the video had exploded. People were celebrating that someone had finally taken charge to bring Tyler down. Some posted that he'd been blackmailing them and lied about having a daughter. It was one thing after another. Most of the packs were celebrating, except for a few. Of course, there was the occasional post about this being staged and not real and that Tyler would spite them all.

The word *spite* made sense in that context, but their threat didn't hinder the hope in over ninety percent of the people's comments. They all hoped and prayed that the dictator was finally going down.

"This is great news." Donovan sighed with relief. "This is what we were hoping for."

"It's way more than what I hoped for." Athan grinned. "This exceeded my expectations."

"Which is a good thing." Cassius nodded and placed a hand on his wife's shoulder. "That proves everyone is desperate for a change in the hierarchy."

"What are the other sites saying?" Were only the wolves rejoicing, or was everyone? That would make a huge difference too.

"Everyone is positive." Katherine clapped her hands. "I can't believe the reception."

"That means we'll have more people willing to fight." Naida gestured around the room. "We'll have more people on our side."

"That's not how things work." Egan frowned. "Even though people are happy, most will still be too scared to act. It's one thing to hope but another to revolt against the person they've considered their leader for so many years."

Like always, Egan and I shared a brain. "Most will be too scared to join us, and the ones who aren't, shouldn't. I'd hate for them to be standing next to us if Tyler comes out of this unscathed."

"Do you expect him to manage that?" Naida's lips parted. "You have the fae on your side, after all."

Ah, there's the elitist fae attitude shining through. "Tyler has a scrappy way of flipping the cards in his favor. You should never underestimate him."

"Though I do tend to agree," Titan said, "I don't see how he could bounce back from this unless he has true blackmail over most of the leaders."

"Maybe." Mom clicked her tongue. "But I agree with Sadie. It'll be less complicated if we remain on our current path. If we add anyone to the mix, we won't know where their true loyalties lie anyway."

"Right." Lillith tapped her finger against her chin. "They could be a mole for all we know, and others could find our location."

"There is one thing we can do." Julie lifted a brow as she scanned everyone. "Eat breakfast before it gets cold."

That reminded me... The clock read that it was eight in the morning. "We slept for over twelve hours?" It shouldn't have surprised me; it had been a crazy two days.

"Yup." Roxy smirked. "It was probably the whole earth-shattering quickie you two had yesterday. We heard it all the way down here."

I stepped into Donovan's side, not even ashamed that I wanted him to protect me.

"Don't be jealous." Donovan placed his arm around my waist and kissed my temple. "I'm sorry Axel can't do that for you."

"Dude!" Axel exclaimed. "You're my best friend. Not cool."

Roxy lifted her chin. "Just so you know, he can and does."

"Okay." Paul walked over to the refrigerator, opened the door, and pulled out a bag of blood. "Let's eat."

I turned my back on the group and grabbed a plate. "I love getting first dibs." I piled on several pancakes and a handful of bacon, knowing this would make the others spring into action.

"Don't you dare," Roxy said. Her arm brushed mine as she took a plate beside me. "Egan eats the majority of it as is. We don't need two pigs devouring everything and leaving barely any for the rest of us."

I faced her. "Fine, but only if you promise to stop bringing up my and Donovan's sex life."

"You witch." Respect filled her eyes. "You win."

Damn straight I did. Besides Axel and me, food was the most important thing to her. I took a second plate and put half of the food on it. "Donovan, I made you a plate."

He chuckled. "Thanks, babe."

"I swear, you Earthlings are so strange," Naida said, standing by the exterior door.

"They just aren't as uptight as the fae." Egan stayed by the kitchen table, letting the wolf shifters get their food first. He normally finished off whatever was left over. "And there isn't anything wrong with that."

"If you say so." Naida's gaze locked on me. "When you're done, we need to go outside and practice your endurance. It looked like you finally connected with your magic yesterday."

"I did." I sat next to Athan and put my and Donovan's plates on the table. "And I even figured out how to shoot magic and create a small force field."

"Great," Naida said and wrinkled her nose as she watched me stuff bacon into my mouth. "All that stuff comes naturally. I was worried you might be too old for it to happen. Every fae has to work on endurance and tele-porting."

At least, that meant I wasn't severely different magic-wise from them. "I'm excited to learn."

"Good." She motioned to my food. "Hurry and eat so we can take off."

That was all the encouragement I needed.

I LED Naida to the same clearing Titan's pack, my pack, Egan, and the vampires had hung out with each other a few weeks back when we'd been getting to know each other and the area.

Donovan wanted to join us, but Naida had put her foot down, saying all he'd do was distract me when I needed all my focus on the task at hand. He wasn't thrilled about staying behind, but he didn't have a valid reason since the fae wouldn't be attacking right then, and if they did, I had the princess to tell them to stand down.

Are you two there? Donovan linked.

Yes. He'd been checking in every twenty minutes since we'd left the mansion. It was cute but getting borderline annoying. I tried to be understanding since the past week had been hell on all of us. *We're getting settled now.*

All right. He sounded unhappy. *Be careful, and let me know if you need me.*

Will do. I love you. Now leave me alone so I can concentrate.

Fine, he groaned before disappearing from my mind.

"Okay." Naida pointed to a tree about fifty feet away. "I want you to channel your magic and hit that tree."

That sounded easy enough. I connected with my magic, and my blood pulsed. The static electricity flowed through my body and down my arm to my hand. The magic condensed under my palm, and I lifted my hand. It shot from my palm and hit the tree right in the center.

When the tree remained unharmed, shock coursed through me.

"Now, maintain the flow," she commanded.

The magic extinguished before I could process what she'd said. "What?" When I shot my magic like that, it was only in short bursts. "Is that even possible without a heads-up?"

"Yes." Naida frowned. "You need to think of your fae magic the same way as your wolf. When things need to change or you need to alter your course, you don't have a problem with it in your wolf form, right?"

"No." I hadn't thought of it like that, but she was right. "If I need to change my attack, I can easily."

"And we need to get you there with your fae powers." She licked her bottom lip and huffed. "We can't get you there before we attack Tyler, but we should get you most of the way."

"How did the tree remain undamaged?" I'd expected it to explode or my magic to cut through it. "I channeled a lot of power at it."

"You didn't wish it harm." She shrugged. "And your magic is part of nature. Even though your magic is fae, your wolf has connected you here, and your magic has adapted to Earth. Just like Fae recharges me, Earth will recharge you."

That was brand-new information right there. "Okay, what do you want me to do now?" I pressed my palms together. "Keep a steady burst on the tree?"

"Let's start with that."

I pushed my magic forward again and concentrated on the tree. As the power left my palm, I pulled upward from my center. With the burst, the magic seemed to bubble and collect before shooting out. With a continuous stream, I'd have to push continually.

Not sure if it would work, I was pleasantly shocked when the stream held steady. It took a lot of concentration to keep it going, but with each passing second, it got a little easier.

She barked out a laugh. "Great! I didn't expect you to succeed on the first try."

Me neither. "What's next?"

"Alternate between shooting small bursts and long steady streams." Naida smirked. "Let's see how that goes."

I shook my arms out and took a deep breath. I had this. I repeated the same process and was able to switch back and forth effectively. I'd never felt so damn proud of myself.

"Let's work on the force field." Naida walked over to a tree about ten feet away. "Put it around you."

I raised my hands to my sides and surged my magic outside of me. Instead of having a focal point, I pushed it out. A pink mist lifted off me and swirled around me. It moved like I was in a snow globe, with sparkles or snow swirling around and around inside.

Naida came closer, and right when she reached the pink mist, the barrier stopped her hand from coming inside. "Good. Now move the field over to me."

The mist began to dissipate.

"No," she said sternly. "Move it from you to me. Lift it into the air and over me."

I should've realized that was what she meant. "Is that possible?"

She crossed her arms, staring me down. "Do you not trust me?"

Pushing more magic out to regain the barrier, I forced the pink haze upward. Naida was at least four inches shorter than me, so it would be harder to get it over my head.

As the force field slowly rose, the magic began to peter

out. When it reached my shoulders, I was sure I couldn't hold it any longer. "I can't ..."

"Keep steady." Naida stepped toward me. "You should get a second wind if you push through the fatigue."

That sounded easy, but I could barely find the magic inside me anymore. I pushed harder and harder, but it remained at shoulder level. The magic began to fade. "I ... can't." I felt like a failure as I released my hold on my power.

Naida's shoulders dropped, and she touched my arm, pushing some of her power inside me. She warned, "Never let anyone but me do this. By letting someone's magic enter you, it can allow them to drain you."

"I'm already drained." She'd seen with her own eyes how I'd struggled. "So I'm not sure what you're trying to accomplish."

Her power mixed with mine, and I felt a boost.

"I'm giving you a little jump-start. In a couple of hours, you'll be fully charged on your own." She dropped her hand and lifted a brow. "But before we leave here, I want you to try one more thing."

"Which is...?"

"I want you," she whispered and nodded to the tree I'd shot power at earlier, "to teleport over there."

I'd done that with the vampire who'd attacked me but never on purpose. In fact, I hadn't done it since then. "How do I do that?"

"Instead of channeling your magic outward, you channel it inward with a location in mind." Something strange reflected in her eyes. "We need to see what powers you have the most control over, so this is the last test."

Exhausted didn't even cover how I felt. We'd only been out here for minutes, but it felt like I'd run a marathon. If this was what I needed to do to get back to the mansion, then I'd try it. I closed my eyes and yanked the small flicker of magic left inside me. I channeled it inward as she'd instructed, and a buzzing feeling brushed across my skin. As the feeling increased, I opened my eyes to find that the clearing had disappeared and blackness had engulfed me.

CHAPTER EIGHTEEN

The darkness suffocated me. I blinked, but my surroundings remained black. My skin still tingled as I tugged the magic inside me even more.

My surroundings closed in on me, and sweat pooled under my armpits. What the hell had I done? I was pretty sure this wasn't supposed to happen.

Donovan popped into my head, causing my paranoia to spike. What if I never got to see him again? I locked in on the image and used it to keep me focused.

A breeze from God knew where blew across my face. I started and blinked as the surrounding air flickered into a scene of familiar trees.

Sadie. Donovan linked with me. *Are you okay? Naida said you teleported and should be here.*

I'm ... I didn't know how to explain where I was. The picture stabilized around me as my feet sank onto solid ground. *... right outside the mansion.* Naida was there, waiting.

"I told him you were fine." Naida rolled her eyes. "But they refused to listen."

We're heading back, Roxy answered me.

"What the hell happened?" I'd never been that scared before. "I was, like, trapped."

"You figured out how to teleport." Naida shrugged like it was no big deal. "Every fae has gone through that."

"A little warning would've been nice." I took a menacing step toward my aunt. "I thought I wouldn't be able to get out."

"You were stuck but not for long." Naida crossed her arms. "Should I have told you that you could get trapped in the space between realms until your magic figured out how to move you?"

"Telling me to move a few feet away made it sound relatively easy." I gestured to the mansion. "This is at least four miles away."

"Places you have an emotional connection to are easier to reach than ones you don't." Naida shook her head. "That's why the day I teleported you and Katherine down one level in the stairwell when the guards were after you took more out of me than returning to the fae realm—another dimension."

Running footsteps pounded toward us. By the sounds of it, Donovan, Roxy, and Axel had been out looking for me.

Naida dropped her arms and mashed her lips. "Look, I'm sorry if it came off like I was tricking you. I didn't mean to. I just hoped it wouldn't happen if I didn't put it into your mind."

"Put it into my mind?" She would have to explain herself better than that.

"What is it you humans say?" She snapped her fingers and tilted her head back. "Psych you out. I thought maybe you wouldn't have an issue if I didn't tell you about it."

I guessed that made sense when she put it that way. "You thought I could travel the short distance?"

"No." She rubbed her fingertip along her lip. "I knew you'd show up here. That's why I came straight here as soon as you disappeared. I honestly assumed you would be worn out and lying here on a recliner." She motioned to the wooden sun chairs on the deck.

My three pack members broke through the tree line and into the backyard. Donovan rushed over to me and pulled me close to him. He rasped, "Every time I turn around, you're in danger."

"Every time?" I tried to make light of the situation. "I'm standing right here, right now."

The fatigue hit hard, and my legs buckled underneath me. Luckily, his arms were already around me and kept me upright.

"Girl, that was awful." Roxy snorted. "You can't say that and then not be able to stand on your own two feet."

Axel ran a hand through his buzzed hair. "I'm still confused about what happened."

Donovan glared at Naida. "I'll tell you ..."

There was no way I'd allow her to take the blame. Maybe she'd been misguided, but her intentions had been noble. "I got stuck between locations for a second, that's all."

"That's all?" Donovan gawked. "That sounds like a big issue."

I forced my legs to straighten so I could support myself. "I'm learning how to use magic."

Roxy cut her eyes at me. "Besides, Naida was out here waiting on her. It's not like she abandoned Sadie." *You owe me.*

The little traitor, but having someone backing me

would help Donovan to cool down. *Oh, no. I've done similar things for you before. Remember that time your dad caught you sneaking out of the house, and I explained to him that we were only going outside to watch the moon for extra credit in science class?*

Don't even. She lifted her chin. *We were supposed to be going to a party, but you made all that noise, so we got caught and were forced to watch that stupid lunar eclipse.*

But your dad was so happy with you. I wouldn't even deny it. I'd hated going to parties and would do anything to get out of them. Everyone had just wanted to use me to get close to Tyler. *He even let you borrow the car to go to the movies on a school night.*

"She was doing so well." Naida grimaced. "But maybe I should've prepared her more."

"Dude," Axel said gently to his best friend. "She's not lying."

"Still not good enough." Donovan snarled. "What would've happened if she couldn't get back here?"

Naida wiggled her fingers. "I gave her magic a jump-start with my magic, so I could've tracked her down."

"See, she had it handled." Axel cringed but kept his tone upbeat.

I was way too damn tired for all of this. "Look, I'm going to go take a nap. Let me know when lunch is ready." I entered the house and didn't bother looking back.

———

THE NEXT TWO weeks passed in a blur. Naida and I trained every day, and with each session, I lasted longer and longer. I had almost complete control over my magic but still struggled with teleportation.

She'd explained that I'd done it with the vampire because my friends had been under threat. I'd managed to use the power, but it wasn't guaranteed to work like that most of the time. That day, I'd gotten lucky.

I grabbed a plate of lasagna and sat at the dinner table between Egan and Donovan.

"Something isn't right." Egan sat at the table, waiting for everyone else to get their food and settle in. "I expected to hear something from Tyler after everything went down. It's been two weeks, and he hasn't made a move."

Titan sat across from the dragon. "He's keeping a low profile and trying to get all the videos taken down. Another alpha I talk to said no one is returning his calls. But Mike from Chattanooga is still hanging around him. They're back at Tyler's Nashville home, trying to do damage control."

"Tyler always reacts," Mom said and dropped her plate hard on the table. Small drops of marinara sauce splashed up and hit Titan's white shirt. "The fact that he hasn't done something drastic scares the shit out of me."

"Maybe he has and we don't know it." Naida sat at the end of the table and stuck a fork in her bowl of kiwi, strawberries, grapes, and cantaloupe. "We are kind of secluded."

That hit hard. "Then why wouldn't Titan's contact alert him?"

A string of melted cheese hung off Roxy's plate. She picked the piece of cheese off and put it in her mouth as she joined us. "Maybe they don't know either."

"He lives in Mount Juliet, right outside Nashville, so closer than us but still pretty removed." Titan scratched his nose. "It's a possibility."

Lillith sat at the bar with Katherine and her siblings. The gothic vampire looked at her father. "What about you, Dad?"

"I haven't reached out to anyone." Cassius sat at the other end of the table and took a large sip of his blood. "I try to stay off the vampire radar, but I could call a friend and see if they have any updates."

Dawn patted her husband's hand. "Why don't you do that? It might help us all relax."

Now that everyone had gotten their food and drinks, Egan stood and piled his plate full of the remaining food.

Katherine watched him layer food on top of more food. "I swear I have never seen anyone eat like that."

"That's because you've never been around another dragon before. We all eat a ton." He winked.

"You eat more than the other ones I've been around." Naida tilted her head. "Which means you're strong."

"Wait ..." Luther set his cup on the island. "Are you like one of the strongest dragons in the world?"

"There are many definitions of what *strong* means." Egan cleared his throat, picked up a piece of buttered French bread, and stuffed it into his mouth.

He'd always been secretive, but we didn't have time to focus on that. We'd pull the truth out of him eventually—after we'd resolved our current situation. For now, I'd help my dear friend out by changing the subject. "Is there someone else you can call?" I asked Titan.

Mom grimaced. "I hate to bring it up, but Brock bit you. Are you not getting a read on him?"

Donovan growled low.

"When we left the condo, I shut that connection down." I didn't want to open it back up, but maybe I should if there was something I could glean from it.

"I get that." Roxy inhaled sharply. "I would never want to feel that asswipe."

Lillith bumped her shoulder into Katherine's and whispered loudly, "Ah, there's my eloquent friend."

"Eloquent?" Naida's face scrunched in disgust. "You consider that eloquent?"

Standing at the island between Luther and Julie, Paul chuckled. "No, that was sarcasm."

"What a relief." Naida exhaled and placed a hand on her chest.

In the past few weeks, I'd learned that she was just as dramatic as Roxy in what you'd consider a fae way.

I steadied myself as I prepared to open the link to Brock. The thought turned my stomach, but maybe this would be a good thing. The longer I waited, the harder it would be for me to even consider doing it. I'd have to rip it off like a Band-Aid.

I removed the barrier, and his emotions flooded into me. That was the one nice thing about him biting me: I could feel him, and he couldn't feel me, just like Donovan could feel all of my emotions. It was probably why he'd freaked out when I'd gotten lost the second time I'd teleported.

When someone claimed a person, they were all-in, and in wolf form, that meant they were privy to your feelings.

The combination of his feelings—anger, resentment, and a desire to prove himself—confused me. That last one worried me most. Something big had to be happening for me to feel him so strongly. "Something's up. We need to find out what."

"Roxy." I hated to ask her to spy on Tyler, but her family was still part of Tyler's pack. "Can you call your parents?"

"Yeah." She pulled her burner cell phone from her pocket. "I haven't talked to them in a while because I didn't want to answer their questions and risk them getting caught in a lie. But what the hell? If they are in danger, I need to know." She dialed her parents.

Everyone became quiet as the phone rang over and over on their end.

It was strange. Her parents always had their phones near in case one of their kids called. It had been a running joke between Roxy and me because there were a few times she'd hoped they wouldn't answer, and they always did without fail.

Roxy looked at me. *What if something's wrong?*

On the fifth ring, someone finally answered.

"It's about time," Roxy snapped. "The one time I want you to answer immediately, you almost let me go to voicemail."

"Roxy, Roxy." Tyler's deep, hate-filled voice came over the line. "You should know better than to speak to your alpha like that."

My friend's pale face somehow turned whiter. "You aren't my alpha."

"Semantics." Tyler chuckled dryly. "You will be one of mine again soon enough."

"Where are my parents?" Roxy demanded.

"Wherever I want them to be," he said coldly. "Now put Sadie on the phone."

"She's not here." Roxy's face was set with determination. "So no can do."

"I know you're lying," Tyler said darkly. "Put her on the phone or I'll have fun with someone in your family." He paused. "Hmm, who should it be?"

There was no way I could let that happen. I stood and took the phone from her. "What do you want?"

"Retribution." His words were barely audible through his growl. "You embarrassed me, burned down my home, and made me the laughingstock of the shifter community."

"No, you did most of that all on your own." If he thought he could upset me like he used to, he would learn differently. "I only helped our community by giving them a chance to have a say in their own lives."

"Is that what you think you've done?" he spat. "No, you've created chaos. But don't worry, I'll be back on top again. These past two weeks, I've been forming an army, and now since we've talked, my plan begins."

"You honestly think you can survive this?" He had lost his damn mind. Even with an army, they couldn't make everyone cower. "How do you figure that?"

"Because you've given me the perfect opportunity to prove to everyone that no matter what gets thrown my way, I'll rise above it." He laughed maniacally. "But first, we have a few housekeeping items to take care of."

My heart dropped. That was how he talked to someone before he took them out. "And what would those be?"

"You need to come back here and tell everyone that the video was a sick joke," he said slowly. "And that I still have the knowledge and information needed to be an effective leader."

"You mean dictator." I refused to allow him to paint a different picture than the reality.

"They're one and the same."

"And then what?" I wanted to see what he said.

"I kill you." He spoke the words with the same cadence someone used to say I love you. "They need to see that I will punish even my own family when they betray me."

"You expect me to just show up and play along?" I'd always suspected he was insane, and this solidified it.

"Yes, because I'm going over to your little plaything's

old pack to find out who took him and the other guy to the orphanage. While I'm there, I'm going to kill one person every hour until you show up."

"You wouldn't." But I knew he definitely would.

"The clock starts ticking now." He chuckled. "You better drive fast."

The line went dead as my world crashed all around me.

CHAPTER NINETEEN

"**N**o." Donovan shook his head, emphasizing his intentions. "We're not going."

"You'd let countless people die?" I still held the phone to my ear, stunned by Tyler's threat. I shouldn't have been, but it was hard to process that this was the man who had raised me if you could even call it raised. "And from your parents' pack too? We can't have that. That has to mean something." I know it meant something to him, but he also wanted to protect me.

Naida stood. "If we're doing this, I need to go back to the fae realm and gather fighters to aid us in this endeavor."

Sometimes, she sounds like she isn't from our current day. Roxy linked with me. *I mean, it sounds cool.*

Egan gives off the vibe too. Not necessarily through his vocabulary but more through his actions. He was a rare gentleman in a world full of douchebags. He treated everyone with respect and kindness, except for those who didn't deserve it. *It must be due to their heritage.* Even though I was half-fae, I hadn't been raised that way.

"Yes, we will need all the help we can get." Titan set his

fork on his plate and winced. "I should've realized he'd do this. I can't let that pack suffer any more than they already have."

"Fine. I will meet you there. I can find you through Sadie," Naida replied and disappeared.

"Honey, it wasn't your fault," Mom assured Titan as she patted his hand. "You were young and trying to protect your pack.

"That's the thing." Titan frowned. "They should've become my pack. I should've stood up to Tyler and not let him take over." He sighed. "Maybe if I had, he wouldn't have gotten into the position he's been in and none of this shit would've happened."

"I think you're oversimplifying it." Egan pushed the plate of food away. "The main reason he gained his position is because he had the blueprints. The very ones that are gone now."

"He's right." We had to get Titan's head out of his ass before he did something stupid. "This is the first time you've been able to do something. He never would've allowed you to leave with that pack, and your pack would have fallen under his control too."

Cassius assured his friend. "There is nothing to feel guilty about."

"Right now, we need to focus on our next steps." The longer we took, the more people would die. "What do we need to do to go?" I had completely lost my appetite and wanted to leave now.

"I'll go back to the house." Titan stood and headed to the door. "We should be ready to leave in thirty minutes. My pack is already gathering and organizing transport."

"I'm going with you." Mom's forehead lined with worry as she looked at me. "Have your cell phone on.

I'll let you know when we're about to load up and pull out."

"Okay." I nodded.

The others followed suit, and then we all dispersed to our rooms to prepare.

As Donovan and I entered our room, he turned toward me. He took my hand and avoided my eyes. "Maybe you should stay here and the rest of us go."

"You can't be serious." I pulled my hand from his, unable to believe my ears. "There's no way I'd agree to that. What Tyler's doing is personal to us. What would you say if I asked you not to go?"

"I just ..." He ran his fingers through his hair and plopped onto the bed. His face scrunched in pain. "I don't want to lose you."

"I don't want to lose you either." My heart thawed. His desire for me to stay behind had nothing to do with him thinking I was weak. That was always where my mind went to first—a product of my upbringing. I walked over to him and placed my hands on his shoulders. "But we're in this together. We're a team, right?"

"Of course we are," he whispered. He lifted his head and kissed me. "Now let's get battle-ready."

———

Around two in the morning, we finally pulled onto a hidden side road. I hated that it had taken us that long, but we lived, at best, five hours away. From what Titan had explained before we'd left, these woods would get us to Donovan's and Axel's parents' pack. We were going to sneak in instead of announcing our arrival.

We had nine vehicles we needed to hide.

Donovan pulled up right behind Titan, so close that the front of our car touched the other car's bumper. Titan, Mom, Torak, and a guy from their pack got out and scanned the area.

"Are we ready for this?" Roxy asked from the backseat of Cassius's Honda Accord. "Do you think my parents are even here?"

"I'm not sure." I opened the door and climbed out of the car. "But we'll find them one way or another. I promise."

I still can't believe Cassius and Dawn insisted on coming. Donovan glanced at the large van behind us that Egan, Cassius, Dawn, Katherine, and Lillith had ridden in. *I figured they'd have stayed back with Julie, Paul, Luther, and Athan.*

Katherine's family had stayed behind since Luther and Athan weren't settled enough with their vampires. They didn't want to risk the two boys losing their humanity. I couldn't blame them.

Another six cars contained four shifters each. Our side had a total of thirty-seven without the fae.

We congregated and waited for directions. Titan would take lead on this one since he was the only one with insider knowledge. None of us had ever visited this pack before.

"Is everyone ready?" Titan asked and waited for everyone to turn their attention on him. "From here on out, we only communicate nonverbally."

"What's the plan once we get there?" It wasn't like our whole group could stay together while trying to save every-one. We'd have to split up to be effective.

"We'll split up." Something like respect shone in his eyes. "You and Donovan will stay with me and your mom." He gestured to Roxy and Axel. "Those two can go with Torak and Joe." And then grouped Egan, Katherine, and

Lillith with two men from his pack, and Cassius and Dawn with another two. Titan continued, "That way you'll all be with some of my pack members, and they'll keep you in the loop. Follow their lead."

That made sense. Titan had twenty-eight pack members versus my four. "Okay." I wanted to argue about being stuck with Mom, but she'd lose her head if we weren't together. Titan was ensuring she stayed rational.

"Okay, let's go." Titan motioned forward.

Mom hugged me. "Honey, please stay close and don't do anything stupid."

"You don't have to worry." I always tried to be smart. "I don't plan on going anywhere."

The air remained stink-free, which helped my case. I wasn't lying.

Mom spun on her heel and took off after her mate. We needed to stay close with our groups, so I rushed forward with Donovan right behind me.

Everyone else filed in, and our group remained quiet. We'd all brought extra clothes to change into because shifting was inevitable. We went slower than necessary to stay under the radar. Wolves had keen senses, and we didn't want to give ourselves away.

The trees thickened, and the farther we went, the more the adrenaline pumped through me. I expected a group of wolves to find us at any second and for the fight to start. So far, we'd been lucky, which made me more anxious. It was too quiet, which meant something big would be going down soon.

We continued for another twenty minutes, and the trees began to spread farther apart. We were getting close to the neighborhood, and the tension around us was thick.

No one knew what to expect. He could have hundreds

of people there or thousands. I doubted it was the latter, but Tyler always liked to err on the side of caution.

I sniffed, looking for an indicator of what was to come. There was no scent of other shifters, which was odd. Normally, at least one person would've been out in the woods in the past day, so the slight scent of shifter should have been around here somewhere. Something was wrong, confirming my worst fears.

Titan stopped and gestured to me and Donovan to follow him. Our large group split into the previously established smaller ones.

We went right for a little while before heading forward again. We were walking no faster than a human, and I spotted standard middle-income homes through the trees. The vinyl siding sagged on a few houses, and the neighborhood had a uniform appearance of grays, yellows, and blues.

Do you see anything? Donovan had half a foot on me. Maybe I was missing something. *I don't see a single person.*

I don't either. Donovan tensed and stepped beside me. *It's like they aren't here.*

Tyler wanted me here, so the answer was clear: they didn't want us to know how many fighters they had until we were in too deep and unable to retreat. *Don't worry. They're here. It's nighttime, so the pack is asleep or confined to their rooms while the guards hide from view.*

At the edge of the woods, Titan stopped in his tracks. A vein bulged in his neck, revealing how stressed he was. He knew, like Mom and I did, how capable Tyler was, even when backed into a corner.

We stood in silence, waiting for something ... anything. Titan had to be coordinating our next move with his pack members.

An owl hooted nearby, scaring me to death.

Great. This would go downhill fast if that was all it took to alarm me.

I glanced left as another group came into view one hundred yards away. I looked right, noticing another group. I'd been right. Everyone was getting into position.

Titan glanced at us and took a long, deep breath. He blew it out and gestured for us to go ahead.

It was time.

As I stepped from the trees, I felt naked. Nothing hid us, and if one person looked out their window, the fight would begin. It was inevitable, but I struggled with the realization. We were at war, but it had taken until this moment for me to truly understand what that meant.

Blood would spill, and people would die.

There was no getting around it. The right question was: Who would make it out alive?

Each step brought us closer to our impending doom. I prayed to God my friends and family would be spared. I'd die in their place if necessary.

We were halfway between the woods and the first house when a door creaked open.

I almost thought I'd imagined it. *Did you hear that?*

Yes. Donovan caught up and walked beside me. *It's about to go down. Don't leave my side.*

No problem. I didn't want to. I needed to keep him and my mom safe. I'd tap into my fae side as soon as it was needed.

Speaking of fae, where the hell were Naida and the others? She'd said they would be here.

We continued forward but slower. I could see a few groups, and we were all moving at the same speed.

A gunshot rang through the air, and I watched in horror as one of Titan's pack members dropped to the ground.

"Larry!" a shifter yelled as he fell to his knees beside his injured friend. "It's going to be okay." The shifter touched his friend's neck and sobbed loud and low.

He was dead.

No, this wasn't a fair fight, which was exactly what Tyler wanted.

Another gun fired, and I heard the bullet heading toward us. Somehow, I knew Donovan was the target. It was his grandfather's pack, so Tyler would want him dead.

I grabbed Donovan's arm and pulled him down right as a bullet grazed his bicep. It felt like everything moved in slow motion until we hit the ground.

"Dammit," he groaned, clutching his wound. "That nicked me."

"If you hadn't moved, it would've lodged in your arm." Probably in a main artery. The gunman was good and knew what he was doing.

Mom crawled over to us. "We're sitting ducks."

That was a very accurate description. Even flat on the ground, we were in the open. Nothing obscured us, and we were easy targets.

We needed to move our position from defensive to offensive. I frantically searched the area, hoping for a solution to come to light.

My eyes flicked to the house between our group and the one on the right and locked on a back window that was cracked open. The barrel of a gun peeked through the opening, aimed in our direction.

Oh, hell no. That wouldn't happen on my watch.

I connected to my magic. After training with Naida for the past fourteen days, my magic was becoming a part of me like my wolf. I pulled the magic toward my hand and opened my palm.

I had to shoot first.

Pink magic shot from my hand and barreled straight for the gun. I watched as it absorbed into the metal, and a loud scream rang out.

Before I could celebrate that I'd hit my mark, doors opened in countless houses, and people ran from every direction toward us. The footsteps turned into paws pounding the ground.

Titan turned to Donovan and me and growled, "Donovan, shift. We don't have time to spare."

Twenty wolves broke through the houses we were standing in the middle of, and all hell broke loose.

CHAPTER TWENTY

I couldn't handle all these shifters on my own. If twenty shifters were attacking our group, the same number was likely heading toward every other group too. That meant there were over one hundred and fifty enemy shifters to our much smaller number.

We needed the fae's help. Where were they?

Bones cracked as Donovan, Titan, and Mom shifted. They wanted me to stay in human form for my fae magic, but dammit, my wolf surged forward, wanting to fight beside them.

Forcing her back, I connected to my magic again, ready to battle. There had to be a way to gain the upper hand.

I surveyed the area. Every shifter was in animal form except for me. Wings flapped in the distance as Egan's huge dragon form ascended.

At least, we had the dragon on our side. That should increase our odds, though not enough. If we survived this, it would be by pure luck.

The wolves were in striking distance. Two attacked

Mom, forcing Titan to pay attention to her instead of the five locked on him.

Donovan growled as he stepped in front of me to protect me. *Act weak until we need you to blow them away. They don't know what you're truly capable of. They'll think you can only do what you did back at the condo.*

That might work. They'd been hiding when I shot the gunman. If I played it off right, maybe they'd think I was exhausted from the amount of power I'd already used. Thankfully, they didn't carry any iron. We'd only learned about the iron after days of research in old books, something Tyler would never bother to do. He'd think he was too powerful and that research was unwarranted.

My body protested as I sagged my shoulders. Everything inside me stayed alert, ready for action.

The remaining thirteen headed straight for us. Their eyes locked on me. It was clear they'd been directed to either kill me or take me to Tyler. Neither option was ideal.

Donovan stiffened and bared his teeth at the enemy wolves, making it clear he wouldn't cower to them.

Five wolves veered straight for him, and the others headed in my direction. The cayenne scent of fear wafted off them.

They were afraid to attack me after the rumors of what I could do. If they were already fearful of just hearing about my fae side, I couldn't wait to see their reaction once they saw what I was capable of. If they all felt that way, that could be our strategic advantage. I wished I could talk to Titan and his pack. I hoped they could play it by ear.

A yelp came from Titan as the five wolves descended on him. One sank its teeth into his front right shoulder, already injuring him.

No, the fighting had just begun, and we already had one

injured and one dead. If this was any indication of how the fight would go, we were screwed.

Mom turned her back on her attackers and watched her mate fall to the ground. The two enemy wolves were about to pounce. I couldn't wait any longer.

I had to use my magic now. I tugged it forward, letting the power pool under my palms. I lifted them, and the magic shot at the wolf on top of Titan. I hit him once then twice before he released his hold on Titan and his legs gave out. He dropped and his eyes rolled back in his head.

That was one down. I turned my attention to the one who'd leaped at Mom and shot at him. Instead of using a sudden burst, I kept the magical flow going. "Bend down," I shouted.

Luckily, all three understood, and I spread each hand farther apart to hit every enemy wolf standing in the way. One by one, they crashed to the ground, either dead or passed out—I wasn't sure which. I had to push my disgust away. We were at the point of either being killed or killing, and I had to protect everyone I could.

The wolves retreated toward the neighborhood.

I'd scared them off, but I wasn't sure if they'd run away or regroup and come back stronger.

Donovan linked with me. *Is something wrong?*

No. I didn't want to worry him. *It's just stress. There are so many.*

And you just kicked twenty of them in the ass. Donovan sounded proud. *Don't give up.*

He was grossly misstating my effectiveness, but he was sweet for trying. I'd gotten lucky.

A pained howl came from the other side of the neighborhood. Someone was hurt, and Titan growled, confirming it was someone on our side.

Egan roared in the sky as he flew toward the noise. Smoke billowed from his mouth, but he didn't spray fire. That was the problem with Egan's magic. It was destructive, especially in the woods. He had to hold back to prevent collateral damage.

A few doors opened, and someone yelled, "Dragons exist?"

I ran toward the houses. If people were being held prisoner, we needed to save them. Maybe they'd join our side and help us fight this vicious army.

The dragon landed, and each step shook the ground. I could only see the side of him as he helped whomever was injured.

Good. One less person I had to worry about. I hit the road that connected the houses and scanned each one. A few people watched from their windows, and a boy stuck his head out the front door of his house.

It was clear from here that these people had been beaten down. There was no telling what kind of wrath Tyler had taken out on them, especially since Donovan and Axel had resurfaced. He would punish this pack since Donovan and Axel weren't available for punishment.

A howl pierced the sky as the fighting continued. From my new location, I could see more of our groups, and it wasn't pretty. Our group was bleeding more than the enemy, which wasn't surprising. We needed help.

I let the magic rub inside me and turned my eyes on Roxy and Axel. They had ten wolves locked on them.

I linked with Donovan, not wanting him to be alarmed. *I'll be right back.*

His displeasure permeated from the bond. *Just be careful.*

Remembering what Naida had said, teleporting to my

best friend and her mate would be the fastest way. They were at least two hundred yards away.

My skin buzzed, and everything around me went black. Then I found myself standing right beside them.

Thank God it worked.

Get down, I commanded them. When they dropped, I pushed the magic forward and out through my hands. I hit the wolves closest to us before picking them off. My focus stayed on them as I hit each one. My magic was depleting, so I needed to conserve it as much as possible.

As I hit the sixth wolf, the smell of musky shifter hit my nose. It was thick and strong and close. I turned around and came face to face with two wolves that had snuck in behind me. They were within striking distance. I lifted my hand to hit them, but the darkest one lunged right at me.

Its body hit me in the chest, and I fell onto my ass. Pain shot up my spine, and I lost my connection with my magic. Before I could focus on my power, the wolf's front paws landed on my chest, pushing me backward. My back hit the ground, and I lost my breath.

The wolf chuckled as he lowered his head to my neck. I wasn't familiar with his scent, so he couldn't be from Tyler's pack. Who had he recruited to take me out?

It was obvious that Tyler wanted me dead now that his little secret was out. I'd hoped I meant more to him than that. He'd watched me grow, but it didn't matter. He was a cold, hard son of a bitch.

The enemy wolf's head lowered to my neck, and I grabbed his throat, keeping him at arm's length.

Sadie! Roxy cried, and something heavy dropped with a loud thud.

I had a feeling it was her. Someone had cut her off when she'd tried to help me, but I couldn't turn my head to check on her. If I did, I'd lose the battle with the wolf. My arms were already screaming in pain.

Another wolf headed toward me, and I knew I was screwed. I couldn't connect with my magic because every bit of my focus was on surviving.

Donovan. Axel linked to his best friend. *Sadie needs help. I can't get to her. More wolves are heading this way.*

My mate responded immediately. *I'm on my way.*

My arms shook. The enemy wolf had at least a hundred pounds on me, and I couldn't hold on much longer.

Screams of agony echoed everywhere. I wasn't sure who they belonged to; there were so damn many. Things were bad, and any hope of winning faded away.

My arms began to give out, and the wolf's mouth lowered to only inches from my neck. His hot, rancid breath hit my face, and he opened his jaws wide, ready to tear at my skin. The wolf was desperate to kill me, probably to prove something to Tyler.

The seriousness of the situation wasn't lost on me. Tyler would get his stranglehold on the supernatural community back. Everything we'd done and sacrificed had been in vain. It would have broken my heart if my rage hadn't taken over me.

Adrenaline pumped through me, strengthening my arms again ever so slightly. Donovan's familiar scent hit my nose, revealing he was close, but so was that second wolf. I had to do something fast, or I'd die.

Dizziness overcame me, and my head rolled to the side. I used the last of my reserves to keep the wolf off me, but barely.

Something hit the wolf, and he and the other nearby wolf dropped to the ground.

A familiar voice asked, "Are you okay?"

Her voice was music to my ears. "Yes." No, I'd almost died, but I had to push that aside. I turned my head toward Naida, tears burning my eyes. "What took you all so long?"

"I encountered some unexpected issues." Naida frowned and gestured to the fifty fae behind her. "But we're here now. Go, and remember to only attack the wolves that attack us. There's no other way to know which ones are enemies."

The group behind her took off, already using their magic and making a difference.

Donovan's wolf appeared next to me and checked me over. *Are you okay?*

"Yes, I'm fine." I patted his head and glanced around, seeing where I was needed next.

"You should shift," Naida suggested. "You might be stronger that way."

"But then I can't use my fae magic." I needed to help my pack the best way I could.

"Fine." Naida lifted her hands and hit another wolf hard in the stomach. It crashed into the ground and didn't move. "I've got to go help the others. Alert me if you need help."

That worked. We had a lot we needed to do. I ran toward Axel and Roxy and stopped, waiting for Donovan to catch up. Once we were all together, I linked to them. *Okay, we might have a fighting chance. We need to find Tyler and Roxy's parents.*

Damn straight. Roxy nodded, her red fur moving with the motion. *Axel and I will go check the houses over there if you two want to start here.*

Sounds good to me. He had to be here somewhere. I ran toward the house closest to us and looked inside the window. An older couple sat on the couch, watching the commotion going on outside. A look of pure fear resonated in their eyes as they clutched each other's hands.

House after house, we ran into the same thing. No matter if they were old, young, or a combination, everyone was petrified. There was no telling what Tyler had done to them in the past two weeks. We'd thought it was quiet, but it was clear Tyler had been very active and punishing anyone he could.

We were now on an even playing field against the wolves. We weren't grossly outnumbered, and the fae's magic gave us an edge. Several pack members were injured, but besides Larry, I didn't see any more dead.

We kept moving. As we passed between houses, a coppery sweet scent hit my nose. It was a strange combination and could only come from one supernatural race —vampires.

Over here. I linked to Donovan and followed the scent. *I think one of the vampires is injured.*

You're right. Donovan's voice was strained. *Let's go find them.*

We raced behind the house and found a wolf with its teeth sunk into Katherine's leg. Lillith, Cassius, and Dawn couldn't get to her because they were each fighting their own enemy, but they were holding their own. They were older vampires, so they were stronger, and in this instance, it was easy to tell.

Donovan rushed past me, his eyes locked on the wolf.

A vampire losing blood was dangerous. One reason they needed human blood was to replenish their own internal supply. If we didn't stop the bleeding soon, she'd die.

Donovan tackled the enemy wolf, and he released his hold on Katherine. I ripped the bottom of my shirt up to my navel and dropped to my knees beside her.

"You have no idea how happy I am to see you," Katherine said weakly. "I knew I was done for."

"Not on my watch." I wrapped the cloth around her leg and tied it tightly. "There, that should slow down the bleeding."

"I'm going to need blood." Katherine sighed. "Or I won't make it."

The severity of the situation was very clear. "You aren't dying," I repeated. I looked around and watched as Donovan killed the wolf. He went to assist the other vampires in their fight.

I waited for another enemy wolf to appear. It felt like the fighting would never end. However, none did. What the hell was going on? "I'll be right back." I stood and walked around, trying to figure out where all of the other enemy wolves were. We'd had a constant string of attacks, one after another.

A hand touched my arm, and my heart skipped a beat. Somehow, someone had gotten the jump on me again.

CHAPTER TWENTY-ONE

I spun around to face my attacker, preparing for a fight. As I connected to my magic, I threw a fist at my captor, but then Naida's face came into view. I pulled back my hand right before I would have made contact. "Are you insane?" She had to be for sneaking up on me this way.

"No." She dropped her hand. "I thought you'd smell me."

"I was a little preoccupied." I turned my back on her to determine if anyone else required help.

Donovan and Cassius knocked out the last remaining shifter, and Lillith and Dawn were tending to Katherine.

I looked between two houses to find Titan and Mom running toward me.

"The fighting is over," Naida said gently. "All the wolves have been dealt with."

Dealt with? I didn't like the sound of that. "What do you mean? Did you kill them all?" I got that we had to defend ourselves, but these wolves were only fighting because the alpha will had commanded them to, or they felt like they had no other choice. I understood that lives would be lost, but I hadn't expected everyone to die.

"No." Murray's commanding voice came from behind me.

I spun around to find the king dressed in all white like before. "What did you do to them?"

"Knocked them out." He lifted an eyebrow, and the air surrounding him didn't stink, proving he told the truth. "We do not want to start a war with Earthlings. Our goal is to get to the alpha that killed our brother."

At least, there was that.

Mom brushed her body against my leg. Her blue eyes focused on my face and then looked me over for injuries.

"I'm not injured," I reassured her and linked with Roxy. *Have you located your parents or Tyler?* I would bet money she hadn't, or she would've alerted me.

No. She sounded extremely disappointed. *We looked in every house that didn't have your scent. We're almost back to you.*

Of course, the coward wouldn't be here. He'd be hiding somewhere safe.

Is everything all right? Donovan asked as he trotted over to me. His dark blue eyes contrasted against his jet-black fur.

I answered him out loud so both Naida and Murray would hear. "Tyler isn't here." The words tasted like sour milk.

"Are you serious?" Murray scoffed.

"Yup, he chose not to fight." He probably couldn't risk getting injured ... prick.

A shuffling of feet and paws headed our way. It didn't sound threatening, but it could be a ruse. If these wolves were desperate, they'd do anything to survive.

"Are we sure everyone stood down?" I didn't want to grow overconfident. That was when things fell through the cracks. *Roxy, be careful. Someone is heading toward us.*

I know. She linked back. *We're following behind them. Two guys are helping an older man.*

Are they a threat? Older shifters were still strong and resilient.

No one is fighting anymore, Roxy assured me. *And I promise, there is no way this guy could harm you even if he wanted to. His name is Ted.*

"Yes, every single wolf is passed out," Naida said. "Even when they surrendered, we knocked them out. We didn't want to risk them changing their minds."

Two shifters in human form stepped between two houses while helping an elderly man make his way to us. Roxy and Axel ran past them, the fae, me, and Donovan.

The older man, Ted, looked to be around eighty, balding on the top of his head. The little hair he had was gray. His warm honey eyes had dark bruises around them, and he lifted a hand, showing deep cuts down his forearm. He shuffled closer until he was twenty feet away. Sweat dripped off his face as his gaze landed on me. "You're the girl Tyler tried to pass off as his daughter, yes?"

I nodded, unable to speak to him. To watch him move and talk revealed how much pain the poor guy was in. The two middle-aged guys beside him kept their heads lowered like they were ashamed.

"Tyler told them to kill you." The man's voice broke.

That wasn't new information.

I'm going to kill him, Donovan promised. *Slowly.*

We already knew he ordered them to do this. We had to keep a level head. "He's not here, so how do you know?"

"Because he was torturing me as he told them." Ted

touched his face. The cuts were so deep that it was taking a while for his wolf to heal him. "He found out I saved two little boys here when they were just a few years old after he'd killed their grandparents and parents."

Donovan tensed beside me, and Axel's head jerked so hard it had to have hurt.

"You saved my mate and his best friend?" I'd figured it would have been a woman, for some reason.

"Your mate?" Ted's hand shook as he placed it on his chest. "Are those the boys?" His gaze flicked from Donovan to Axel. "It has to be. Their scents ..."

"Yes, it is." I wanted to hug the man, but I'd only hurt him. "And we have so much to thank you for."

"The only thanks I need is for you to take down that evil tyrant."

"Dad," one of the guys beside him warned. "You can't talk like that. He almost killed you."

"Like hell I can't." The older man's jaws clenched, and anger flared in his eyes. "I'm old, and those boys didn't deserve to lose their families. I'd have kept them and raised them as my own, but Tyler would have figured it out eventually. Their best chance to survive was that godforsaken orphanage. I still dream about that night to this day."

"As touching as this is," Naida interjected, "do you know where the asshole is?"

For once, she sounded like she was from here and not the fae realm. Maybe we were rubbing off on her.

"Yes," Ted croaked. "He went back to his guarded home to stay safe from the fight. The other alpha and his son were with them."

He had to mean Brock and Mike. "Anything else we should know? Do they have a large army with them there too?"

The shifter holding Ted up on his other side said, "No, they don't. I heard whispers when Tyler wasn't around. He left everyone here to fight. He didn't think you'd win even with your fae magic. Granted, he didn't expect an entire fae army to show up at your side. No one is protecting him, and people in his own pack now have reservations. He's the weakest he's been in years."

His lies about me were finally catching up to him. Karma was a bitch, and people didn't like to be forced into things.

"Sadie," Cassius said and walked toward us. "We need to get back to the cars. Katherine needs to replenish her blood before it's too late."

"We need to leave anyway." The longer we took to get there, the more time he'd have to prepare. His guards had likely told him we were defeating them. I glanced at the two middle-aged men and the older one. "We will be back to check on everyone."

"You all be safe. Tyler said he'd be back to finish the job. I'd rather him not, but you do whatever is needed to come out of this alive. I've had a long life as should each one of you." Ted turned slowly, heading back in the direction he'd come.

The man had meant each word, reassuring me that not everyone out there was a complete asshole. Most people were kind and good, thought of others, and were willing to risk their own lives to do the right thing. It was something I'd needed to see.

I watched him walk away for a second before coming back to the present.

"Let's gather our people and take them back home. Our power has already been depleted tremendously. We won't be able to recharge in time for the next battle." King

Murray pointed at his sister. "They don't need us anymore."

Naida shook her head. "I'm going with them. I want to watch him die."

Murray wanted to say something, but Egan's large dragon form flew over the houses and landed right beside us, close to the woods.

I faced Titan. "Tell your pack to meet us back at the car. Katherine's condition will worsen if we don't hurry." It would be a slow process getting her back injured like that. We were all worn out from the fight and couldn't carry her the entire way.

"I'm leaving," King Murray informed us. "Naida, be careful, and let me know when it's been handled."

"Thank you." I wasn't sure if I should say it or not. They'd come here because Tyler had killed one of their own, but if they hadn't, things would've gone much differently.

"Of course." Murray cleared his throat uncomfortably. "You're family, after all." He turned and headed off, looking for his people.

Egan hurried past us to Katherine. When he reached her, he laid his entire body on the ground and glanced at me. He lifted his head, trying to communicate with me.

I hadn't even considered Egan taking her. That would speed up the process and get her to her blood quicker. Just like we had packed extra clothes, the vampires had packed a lot of blood. "Put Katherine on Egan's back." It was only four in the morning, and the sky was pitch black. He'd be able to fly with her to the cars without anyone noticing as long as he hovered close to the trees.

Cassius leaned down and picked Katherine up like a

baby. "Can someone get on top of the dragon and help me get her up there?"

"Yeah." Lillith pursed her lips and looked at the dragon. "How do I get up there?"

I rushed over to help, seeing as all the taller guys were in wolf form. There would be no changing back until we got back to the car and their clothes, so we had to make do.

As I reached Egan's side and scanned his body, a realization settled over me. "I can transport her up there." I'd done it earlier, so this shouldn't be too difficult.

"It's a lot harder to transport someone else." Naida made her way next to me and touched Katherine. "I'll do it. We still need to work on your magic before you try that."

Relief flowed through me. I hadn't been thrilled about doing it and getting us both stuck somewhere while she bled out. "Why don't you go to the cars, then?" That would get her there faster and without issues.

"I can't." Naida frowned. "I'm not sure where they are. This is the safest option."

"Oh God," Katherine groaned, but she didn't remove Naida's hand. "I'm going to puke, aren't I?"

"You didn't last time, so you should be good," Naida said dryly. "Either way, let's go." The fae and Katherine blinked out a few times before they disappeared and reappeared on top of Egan.

"Ugh ..." Katherine moaned. "I'm going to blow."

"Eww." Lillith wrinkled her nose. "Don't do it."

Naida released Katherine, and the vampire slumped over and almost fell off Egan.

"You need to ride with her," Cassius said with concern. "Otherwise, she'll fall off."

"Fine." Naida sighed. "Let's go, dragon."

Cassius, Lillith, Dawn, and I jumped back as Egan's

wings lifted, and he stood on both legs. He shot into the sky before lowering right above the tree line. He flew away, leaving our group alone.

We're ready. Donovan linked. *Titan headed back to the entry point. He's meeting the pack there.*

Our group took off toward the woods, heading back to the cars. As we ran by houses, people stood outside, scouring the area. The two men who had helped Ted were standing outside, keeping the pack calm.

I wondered if Ted was essentially the alpha of the pack. That would be one more reason Tyler had been so eager to get rid of him.

None of that mattered, though. Our focus needed to stay on getting back to the cars and to my childhood home. No matter what I did, it always came back full circle to that place.

We went into the woods, and the scents of Titan and the others were strong. Within a few steps, we found them waiting. As soon as Titan saw us, he howled, and the pack raced back to the vehicles. The alpha waited for Mom, and I went next with Donovan following behind me.

Running was easier and faster, and we weren't worried about making noise or trying to remain hidden. Because of that, we made it back to the cars in half the time.

When the vehicles came into view, I found Egan back in human form, leaning against the van. My eyes went past him and landed on Katherine. She sat in the passenger seat, gulping down a bag of blood. Her eyes weren't as sunken, and she appeared to be doing better.

"I've already got the clothes out." Egan gestured to the pile of clothes on the forest floor.

The wolves already knew what to do as they sniffed the air and ran to their change of clothes. Each one took off into the woods, shifted back into their human form, and got dressed. Donovan was the last one to take off into the woods, but he stayed closest to me.

"Where's Naida?" I'd expected to see her here, but I couldn't find her anywhere, and her scent was slightly old.

"After the fight and teleporting, she decided to go recharge." Egan lifted his hands. "She said she'd meet us at Tyler's."

"Okay." Hopefully, we wouldn't need her again. "Are you okay? Did you get hurt?" I surveyed him for any injuries.

He shook his head. "I'm fine. I did a lot of flying and helped whomever needed it the most." His jaw ticked. "If the fae hadn't come, things might have gone differently back there. That was more than a fight. He wanted to decimate us."

"Thank goodness he's not actually my father. I always worried I'd wind up like him, but I'm no longer worried about that." In an attempt to avoid talking about this anymore, I turned to Katherine. "How are you holding up?"

She slurped the last bit of blood from the bag and licked the excess from her lips. "A lot better. I need another bag or two. Then I should be back in order." She removed the cloth and lifted her leg. "See."

Her injury was scabbed over and no longer a gaping wound.

"Good." I reached into the cooler and handed her another bag. "Drink up."

The wolves trickled out, and within moments, we were all climbing back into the same vehicles and pulling out onto the main road. Tyler's pack was twenty minutes away.

Donovan took my hand and pulled me under his arm. "Do you think Tyler knows we're coming?"

"Without a doubt," Titan answered confidently. "Either a guard alerted him, or someone back there did because they're afraid."

"That's why we need to get there soon." Mom turned toward us.

The truth of her words thundered in my ears.

No leaving me this time. Donovan kissed the side of my head. *With Tyler and Brock there, I need you next to me so I don't lose it.*

That was fair. I could only imagine how he felt. *I promise.* He wasn't being demanding or controlling. He was asking me to help him. He'd gone through hell as he'd watched Brock kidnap me and almost force me into a bond I didn't want. He needed me.

The rest of the car ride passed in silence with each of us gearing up for an inevitable kill. Even though the man had treated me horribly over the years, he had been the one constant in my life beyond Roxy. But if we didn't kill him, so many people would die. He'd already killed too many.

We turned onto a familiar road that headed right into the pack. There was no point in trying to be covert; he knew we were coming and how long it would take us to get there.

The houses came into view, knocking the breath out of me. The pack that I'd foolishly thought wouldn't protect him were all lined up on the road, preventing us from entering.

CHAPTER TWENTY-TWO

I blinked, hoping what I saw was an illusion. When my eyes opened, though, nothing had changed. Fifty of the pack members blocked the entrance to my childhood neighborhood.

"What do we do?" Titan asked uncomfortably. He idled the car only ten feet from the closest person.

Mom turned to me. "Didn't that man say they weren't thrilled with that dick?"

"Yeah." But it could have been hearsay. He was old. For all we knew, he'd misunderstood what he heard. There was only one way to find out. I opened the car door.

"Hey." Donovan caught my hand. "What are you doing?"

"I'm going to talk to them." Otherwise, we wouldn't know where they stood. "It won't hurt."

"You do realize we're down to twenty-seven of my pack members, including Winter and me." Sadness laced each syllable of the alpha's words. "We're outnumbered again."

"If I think it'll come down to a fight, I'll hurry back." I

pulled my hand from Donovan's and placed my feet on the cement. "I'll stand by the car." Not waiting for them to raise any other concerns, I stepped out of the car but left the door open. It was my fail-safe in case something went wrong.

A guy I'd gone to school with stood right in front. Blake's hunter-green eyes watched me as his ash-blond hair reflected the moonlight, making it appear gray. He was the same height as Donovan but was now slightly less built since Donovan had turned all wolf. "What are you doing here, Sadie?"

"You know why I'm here." We'd grown up together. He'd been a decently close friend in high school, and I knew he hated Tyler. "I should be the one asking you that question. Why are you blocking us from entering?"

"You know why too." Blake lifted an eyebrow. "I don't have much of a choice."

Tyler had always dangled Blake's mom's poor health in front of him. It was the main reason for his immense disdain. His mom had gotten cancer, despite it being extremely rare among shifters. She'd lived a decent life the past ten years because Tyler had covered the medical expenses for all of her treatments. Blake's father was a strong wolf and hated Tyler with a passion. Out of everyone in the pack, he was the only one who could come close to dethroning Tyler. Tyler couldn't have that, and he used Blake's mother as his security blanket. As long as they didn't rise against him, he would continue to pay for her treatments. "Do you think she's even sick?" If I could plant a seed of doubt, that should be all that it would take to get him to help us. The others would follow suit and let us through. Most of the pack members looked at him and his dad as the unofficial authority of the pack.

Something shifted inside him. His confidence disappeared, and he tugged at his ear. "What do you mean?"

There it was. He had his own doubts. All I needed to do was foster it and the fact that I believed every single word helped. "Do you think she's sick, or is he getting a doctor to say that and making her sick?"

"He wouldn't ..." Blake paused and ran a hand down his face. "But what if she is?"

"We can figure it out together." I took a step toward him. "I'll do whatever I can, but if he's doing this to her, there's only one way this ends for everyone."

Mom's car door opened, and she joined me outside.

"Winter?" An older lady gasped and clutched her throat. Her light brown hair fell over her shoulder, emphasizing her reaction. "Tyler said you were dead."

"He's said a lot of things, Char." Mom waved a hand in front of her face. "But you can see that I'm alive and standing here." She glanced over her shoulder at me. "And Tyler has done things like that to many people before. It wasn't just the blueprints he used against everyone. He uses any weakness, and with you, a blueprint wouldn't matter. You were already part of his pack."

"What has he done in the past?" Blake asked with concern.

"For one, Roxy." Mom glanced at my best friend, sitting in the van. "Her father was one of the strongest men in the pack, even on the same level as your father." Mom faced Blake again. "He spoke out against Tyler, and the next thing you know, a red-headed girl was delivered only a few months later."

Red-headed wolves were rare and seen as weak. The unique color lowered the entire family's status since the family was seen as prone to birth defects. Their bloodline wasn't considered strong.

"But it was a witch." Char huffed. "Don't even try to paint it as Tyler."

"Tyler hired her." Mom stepped closer to them. "I overheard him on the phone."

"You're lying," Char spat.

"Does it smell like I am?" Mom leered. "Unless you're telling me your sense of smell is gone?"

"Why didn't you ever tell anyone?" Peter asked and lifted his chin. His cobalt eyes glared at Mom as he rubbed his fingers through his dark brown goatee.

"Because I was pregnant and Tyler didn't let me out of the house." Mom fisted her hands. "But he coerced the witch to curse that family, and when my daughter was born with pink hair, he used the opportunity to blame her for that as well. He acted like he'd saved our pack when he was the one who had caused the problem."

I hadn't expected Mom to give such a passionate speech, but everything she'd said was true.

"He manipulates or kills anyone who gets in his way. Do you want to stand here and protect a man who wouldn't think twice about killing you?" I focused on Blake. He was the one I needed to get on my side.

He blew out a breath. "Fine."

"Are you serious?" Char's head snapped in his direction. "You're letting them through?"

"They're right." Blake glowered. "If we work with them, we can take him down. This may be our only chance. Do we want to give that up?"

My heart raced as I waited to see how the others would respond. This was a pivotal moment. If they joined our side, we wouldn't be outnumbered.

"No." Blake's father stepped forward and stood beside his son. "We need to let them through and do what we've been afraid to do ourselves—end the tyranny."

A few others mumbled their agreement as they stepped aside, allowing us to drive through.

Mom nodded and got back into the car.

As I followed her lead, Blake's dad called, "Sadie."

I stopped and looked at him as he jogged over to me.

What's he doing? Donovan asked, alarmed. *Get in the car. Maybe it's a trick.*

No, it's not. I know him. But it was odd. "What's up?"

He lowered his voice so only Donovan could hear. "Look, some of these people aren't thrilled with me backing Blake, but I think you're right. We've suspected that Tyler is doing something to Marie. This is a risk we have to take, but most of those people are just scared. They all have something to lose."

"That's not surprising." I wanted him to get to the point, but I hated to rush him.

"Someone may have warned Tyler already. He has his most loyal guards surrounding him, and Roxy's parents are being held at the house. Even that other douchebag alpha, Mike, and his son are there with their guards. I'd say there's about forty guards in total."

"Anything else we need to know?" The more we could go in armed the more likely we would succeed.

"No, not really." Blake's dad winced. "I would go with you, but I can't risk anything worse happening to Marie if the fight doesn't go in your favor. Tyler will be angry enough with us letting you through."

"No, I understand." Marie getting injured worse wouldn't be something I'd risk either. Family was way too damn important. I'd learned that recently. "Thank you. You've done more than enough."

"Good luck." He took a few steps back. "We're rooting for you."

I climbed into the car and shut the door. "Did you all get that?"

"Yeah." Titan put the car in drive. "Already alerted my pack."

"Did you let Roxy and Axel know?" I took Donovan's hand and steeled myself for what was to come. Touching him calmed my wolf.

"Apparently, Roxy had her window rolled down and heard the whole thing." Donovan rolled his eyes. "She's a handful."

"Very true." She always had been. "At least you didn't have to deal with her during her dramatic teenage years."

Donovan feigned horror. "Was she worse than she is now?"

I laughed, which surprised me, given our current situation. "Yes, very much so."

"As frightening as that sounds, I hate that I missed all those precious years." Mom's tone took on an edge of sadness. "It still guts me."

Titan slowly followed the road to the back entrance of the neighborhood. He tapped his fingers on the steering wheel. "You're going to tell me how to get there, right?"

"It's easy to spot." Mom pointed down the road and to the right. "Just follow that, and it'll be the largest house on the block. It's hard to miss."

"I figured." Titan followed her instructions. "Tyler tried to get me to come here often, but I always refused. I was always wary of him."

"That's because you're smart." Mom shifted in her seat.

"He's very charismatic, and many people don't realize how big of a snake he is until it's too late."

The house that still haunted me appeared. I'd expected to see some damage from the fire we'd set, but the place looked untouched like it had been a strange dream. "How did he fix it so quickly?"

"I'm sure Mike had something to do with it." Titan pulled right in front and parked the car. "He has more money than he knows what to do with."

I had to at least look at things in a positive light. "His reputation must have taken a hit too."

"Two desperate men trying to reclaim their status." Donovan nibbled on his bottom lip. "Probably not the best thing for us."

And there was the rain cloud over my head, but his point was valid.

The vehicles stopped behind us, and everyone clambered out. Katherine walked strong, already healed. Sometimes, I was jealous that vampires healed much faster than shifters, but it was easier to weaken them. All it took was a deep enough cut to cause a decent stream of blood. We were a little more durable.

We have to find my parents. Roxy's anxiety slammed into me. *I ... I have to make sure they're okay.*

Being this close to them had to be difficult. Before, she'd had no clue where they might be, but here, it was obvious. He'd have them downstairs in the basement near where the blueprints used to be. There was only one way down or up —through the doorway.

Wolf shifters howled and raced around the houses, their sounds getting closer.

Roxy rushed to the front door. *I'm going inside to find them.*

Wait. She didn't need to go in there alone, but I could tell she was determined. Nothing I said would deter her.

Dammit, I had no other choice. "We're going inside." At least the fighters were focused on the threat outside and we shouldn't have many to fight inside.

"Fine, but if you need help, scream." Mom stood with the others, waiting on the wolves to reach them. "And if you aren't out here in ten minutes, I'm coming after you."

Axel, Donovan, and I chased after Roxy, each one of us determined to keep our pack member safe.

When she opened the door without anyone attacking her, that was our first clue that something was off, but right then, there was no reasoning with Roxy.

The house was eerily quiet as she ran down the hallway and threw open the door to the basement.

I was only a few steps behind her and staying close. Any trace of smoke was gone, and we found no one downstairs. Where the blueprint room had been was now a wide-open space with a cement floor. The walls were blocks of cement with chains affixed to them. The scent of blood hung in the air, and there were drops of blood on the floor near where handcuffs were attached to the chains.

My stomach churned. None of this made sense.

"Where are they?" Roxy spun around like she expected her parents to magically appear. "They have to be here somewhere."

"Babe, they aren't here," Axel said slowly. His eyes flicked to Donovan and me for help.

"Then where are they?" she asked hysterically.

That was when it clicked. "The wolves ran from around back. They have to be outside."

If they were outside, that meant they had more backup.

Tyler had held back his numbers in case we were let through.

Donovan, as the last one down, was closest to the stairs. He turned to run up the stairs as I did one final sweep of the area. Something odd caught my eye.

Behind the stack of boxes, I saw a faint outline at the top. It was odd. I'd never seen that before.

Sadie ... Roxy grabbed my arm, dragging me to the stairs. *We've gotta find my parents.*

Look. I dug my heels in and pointed at the wall. *Something's there.* Normally, there was an extra box on top. Someone must have forgotten to put it back.

You're right, Donovan said as he and Axel ran over to move the boxes that were in the way. With each box removed, the outline of a hidden door became clearer.

I'd always thought the basement was only half the house, but what if it spanned the whole damn thing? I could see this horrible family creating a secret lair. Technically, there was a place where they kept and tormented traitors, but what if there was a place for the ones Tyler didn't want anyone to know about?

When the last box was moved, Roxy rushed over and ran her fingers along the door's outline. *How do we get back there?*

No clue. I examined the boxes they'd moved. They weren't dusty like the others, which meant they were regularly moved. The tip of something flat—a piece of metal— stuck out from between the flaps of a box. I squatted, opened the top, and found a long, flat letter opener. Blankets lay underneath.

I grabbed the opener and stood next to Donovan by the door. At the right edge, at about shoulder height, was a slight indentation like someone had used the same place over and over again to open the door. Going with my gut, I stuck the edge of the letter opener into the gap between the wall and door and pushed the handle toward the wall. The door popped open.

The door had been sealed well, and a sewage smell hit me, making me gag. The amount of feces in the air told me that either there were multiple people in there or someone had been in there for a very long time.

Oh, God. Axel waved his hand in front of his nose. *That's rancid.*

That was putting it mildly. I stepped inside the dark, narrow hallway. The walls, ground, and ceiling were pure cement. No wonder it had stayed secure when the fire had raged in the safe room.

I slowly walked through the hallway. A flowery smell mixed in with the foul one, and there was no musk.

Your parents aren't in here. I didn't want Roxy to get her hopes up. I wasn't sure if this was good or bad news.

She must have felt the same way because her emotions neither spiked nor calmed.

I'm right here, Donovan assured me as he stepped close behind me.

It was nice to know I wasn't alone, but the underlying scent smelled fae, which was odd.

At the end of the hallway, I entered a large open room. My gaze went straight to a skinny short man chained to the wall. He was crumpled on the ground, but his lavender eyes, which matched his long, stringy hair, locked on mine. He wore a brown shirt, or maybe it was just that dirty.

Something tugged inside me, and I ran over to the man without hesitation. I touched his wrists as I examined the handcuffs, and something popped inside.

He felt familiar, even more so than Naida. But that

couldn't be. I dropped my hand and looked straight into his bewildered face. I asked quietly, "What's your name?"

The strange man cleared his throat. "It's Rook," he replied hoarsely and tried to scoot away from me, fear in his eyes. "Who are you, and what do you want from me?" he asked in defeat.

CHAPTER TWENTY-THREE

My brain couldn't process what he'd said. Surely, I'd lost my mind. My father couldn't be alive. "I'm Sadie." The words tumbled from my mouth without a thought.

"I've never met you." Rook slowly climbed to his feet. "But your magic is just like mine."

"I ..." I didn't know what to say. We had so much going on. I didn't have time for this. I needed to help find Roxy's parents.

Roxy entered the room and stepped beside me. "She's your daughter. That's why."

"What?" Rook's mouth dropped. "How is that possible?"

Really? Donovan sounded annoyed. *Just blurt it out for her, why don't you?*

I'm sorry. Roxy sounded remorseful. *But we need to speed this up. My parents are in danger.*

She was right. We could do this later. "Winter is my mom. But we need to get out of here. Our people are under attack."

I reached for the restraint, and Rook smacked my hand away.

Donovan growled and rushed to my side. He rasped, "You may be her father, but I will hurt you if you touch her like that again."

"She can't touch that." He lifted his hands, rattling the chains. "It's iron. It'll drain her."

"Wait ..." Dread pulled at my stomach at the thought of Tyler knowing the fae's weakness. "Tyler knows that?"

"No, the witch who helped him capture me did." Rook leaned against the wall, out of breath. "She kept apologizing, and she lied to Tyler. She told him she put a spell on me to hide me. She wanted to give me a chance to escape."

Watching Rook struggle to merely stand hurt. "Donovan, can you get him out?"

Axel entered and held up a small, sturdy wire. "I can do that. Donovan isn't as skilled as I am." He walked over to Rook's chains and began picking the lock. "I figured this might come in handy."

He looked like a pro, which unsettled me, but it also reminded me that even though I felt like I knew these two inside and out, they had a life prior to Kortright University that I didn't know much about. "Where did you learn to do that?"

"We were young and stupid." Donovan grimaced. "Let's just leave it at that."

A faint click sounded, followed by the handcuffs and chains hitting the ground. Rook didn't budge. "Is this a cruel joke?"

"No, it's not." I'd bet that after being imprisoned here for over eighteen years, he didn't want to hope. "But the others need us."

A wolf howled outside, and my skin turned cold. The

sound was a plea for help, which had been my fear. *We need to help him upstairs and get to the others.* Rook would struggle, trying to make it up those stairs by himself.

"Are you ready?" Donovan asked the broken fae. "I can help you up the stairs."

"No." He sucked in a breath. "I'm good. Let's get out there and help your friends."

I wanted to argue with him, but time was limited. *Roxy and Axel, you two go on. Donovan and I will be right behind you.* I wanted to get out there, but I needed to make sure Rook was okay. I couldn't lose him minutes after finding him.

Without hesitating, Roxy and Axel ran out the door.

Rook took off right after them. It surprised me that he kept up. He walked with a limp, but he was right behind them.

Okay. Donovan chuckled. *I didn't see that coming.*

He's probably using all his energy. I wondered how often they'd fed him. Hell, I had no clue how often fae needed to eat. Naida didn't eat much, but she'd sit with us at each meal. The hope of freedom, though, was probably energizing him.

Naida ... where was she? She needed to get here and help me with Rook. Getting him back to the fae realm was a priority. I wasn't sure how to make that happen if she didn't return soon.

Once we hit the hallway, I heard another yelp. They were in the backyard. Axel, Roxy, and Rook turned in that direction.

The fae was determined to stay with us.

"Rook." He couldn't fight like this. "Go out the front door and get in one of the cars."

"I'm not hiding," he said without looking over his shoulder. "I'm going to fight with you." He ran after Axel and Donovan through the back kitchen door.

No! Roxy screamed internally.

I was sure she hadn't meant to do that. Something was very wrong. I rushed out the door, and my feet stopped.

I couldn't believe my eyes.

Tyler, Mike, and Brock were standing in front of Roxy's mom and dad. Her parents were in their wolf forms, chained to a tree. Blood pooled at their feet from where they'd been tormented and cut as if they'd been tortured for answers. Ten guards surrounded them, all in wolf form. The fur on their backs was raised; they were ready to fight.

Tyler must have thought that Roxy's parents knew where we were staying and wanted the information to attack us without warning.

But that wasn't the worst part.

Tyler's eyes flashed with anger when they landed on Rook, and he jerked the hand that held a long, sharp knife. The blood of Roxy's parents dripped off the blade. "How did they find you?"

Rook couldn't fight in his state, so I'd make Tyler focus on me. "You didn't hide him very well." I pretended to be unfazed. He got off on upsetting people to make them think irrationally. "The hidden door's outline was super easy to find." The more I gloated, the angrier he'd get.

"That's fine." Tyler lifted his chin and looked down his nose at me. "I'll get him back." He kneeled next to Roxy's mother and placed the knife against her throat. "But first, you need to watch the show."

"No!" Roxy yelled and stumbled toward them.

"Stay back, or I'll slit her throat." Tyler dug the knife into her mom's throat, and she whimpered. "That won't be nearly as fun, and you can blame her quick demise on yourself."

The surrounding guards inched closer to us, making it clear this would be another battle.

With each win, Tyler became more malicious and heartless. It had to be the cost of gaining power the way he did. I couldn't let him continue.

My wolf surged forward, and I couldn't hold her back. I'd repressed her too long. For years, Tyler had tormented us both, and she wanted retribution too.

My skin rippled as my rose-gold fur sprouted all over and my bones cracked. My body lowered to the ground as my clothes ripped. On all fours, I lifted my head to the sky and howled in warning and celebration. It felt good to be in this form again.

"Do you think that scares me?" Tyler asked and chuckled. "Mike, are you scared?"

"Nope." Mike's forehead was coated with something other than sweat. It had to be the gel melting off his hair. "Just some weak bitch acting like she's stronger than she is."

Rook tensed beside me. "How dare you."

"Oh, shut it, fae," Brock said, but fear shone in his eyes. "We weren't talking to you."

I opened my connection to him and felt pure, raw terror and hate. I wasn't sure who the hate was for.

"Why are you even here?" Donovan snarled. "Do you still want to mate with her since you found out she's his daughter?" He pointed at Rook. "It doesn't give you an advantage now, so leave my mate the fuck alone."

"We don't have much of a choice," Brock snapped and bared his teeth at me. "I claimed her, so she either dies or we complete the bond." The hatred rolled off him.

His animosity was purely for me. Great.

"You won't be doing anything to her," Donovan growled.

We've got to do something. Roxy's desperation clung to her words. *He's going to kill her.*

She was right. Every moment we stood here proved he had power over us. That couldn't be allowed.

Our options were limited. If we moved toward him, he'd cut her deeper, and the guards would spring into action. I should've stayed in human form so I could use my fae magic.

But ... what if I could use it in wolf form? I'd never tried, and Tyler wouldn't expect it.

I glanced at the left side of the backyard, and it looked like we were holding our own. Egan fought ten wolves in dragon form, and the vampires fought five other enemy wolves alongside him. I didn't see any wolves from Titan's pack, which meant they were still fighting in the front yard. Tyler must have had an extra twenty-five hidden back here. I only hoped our close to thirty could hold their own without suffering any losses.

But I had to concentrate. I reached deep inside and felt my magic. I didn't know why, but I'd expected it not to be there. I was fae and wolf, though, and should be able to tap into both.

I connected with my magic and didn't know what the hell to do with it. I didn't have hands to channel it through.

I guessed paws would have to do.

Like in human form, I pushed the magic toward my right paw. When the power bubbled underneath, I lifted it and aimed the stream of pink light at Tyler's chest.

It slammed into him, knocking him onto his back, and the knife dropped at his feet. He wasn't getting off that easy. I kept a steady beam right at him.

The guards sprang into action. One lunged at me and tackled me onto my back. My magic cut off as I landed hard.

Rook rushed in behind me while bones cracked as my pack shifted. If we wanted to be formidable, we needed our animals front and center.

Right now, I had to focus on myself and prevent Rook from interfering. The wolf snapped its teeth inches from my neck. I channeled my magic, making it unruly to the point where my blood boiled. I needed the asshole to burn and get off me.

More wolves surrounded me, their intent clear. Tyler wanted me dead, probably to claim he'd been fooled all these years and he'd taken care of the problem despite raising me as his own like any alpha would've done.

The wolf on top of me whimpered and jumped off, skipping from one paw to the other in pain.

Another enemy wolf crouched, ready to attack, when Donovan jumped on its back and sank his teeth into the back of its neck.

The wolf thrashed to get him off, but he held on tight.

Roxy attacked another, and Axel took on the wolf right beside me. That still left six wolves targeting me.

Dizziness overtook me, indicating the fae had arrived. It wasn't as strong as the other times, but something shifted inside me whenever they appeared.

"Get away from her!" Naida said loudly.

She and Murray materialized on either side of me.

"Nads?" Rook gasped. "Murray?"

They stilled, and Naida spun around like she'd forgotten the danger we were in.

"Rook?" She stumbled. "How are you here?"

"Long story," Rook answered.

A white wolf close to Naida struck. His teeth tore at her

arm, and I slammed into him, throwing him off her before he could do more damage.

"We can do this later!" Murray barked. "Get your head in the game."

Naida spun around, her teal eyes glowing. Anger pulsed from her as she raised her hand and pushed her magic into the wolf that had attacked her.

"Let's get out of here," Tyler whispered.

Oh, hell no. That wasn't happening. My brain focused in a way it had never done before. I didn't need to connect with my magic; it roared inside me but not outrageously like before. I bared my teeth at the enemy wolves surrounding us and embraced the power raging inside.

Murray and Naida lifted their hands, and power exploded from their palms. They knocked the wolves back, creating an opening I had to take. I couldn't let Tyler and dumb and dumber get away.

I raced toward them as Donovan, Axel, and Roxy appeared. I glanced over and found the three wolves that had attacked them dead. I hated that—they'd likely been forced to fight—but we had to protect ourselves.

The four of us pushed our legs hard. They weren't getting away fast since Roxy's parents were in such bad condition. Tyler dragged them behind him by the chains that bound them. They hadn't thought through their escape plan.

"Guards!" Tyler yelled, but no one came.

Egan and the vampires were still fighting the others, and Murray and Naida were taking care of the ones closest to us. They had no help. These cowards would have to defend themselves.

"Fine." Tyler stopped running and faced us. He pulled

a gun from his jacket pocket and aimed it at me. "This is all your fault," he sneered and fired.

I eyed the bullet that barreled toward me and forced it to drop to the ground. I let the magic build inside me and teleported right behind Tyler.

"Where did she go?" Mike asked, bewildered.

Idiots. I jumped on Tyler's back and dug my claws into his skin. I sank my teeth into his neck, and he released his grip on the chains and gun to grab my head. He turned it so my snout pressed right against the skin, preventing me from breathing.

Donovan linked with me. *I'm coming.*

No, I'm fine. Roxy's parents needed help. *Focus on the others so we can get Roxy's parents to safety.* I pushed my magic into my paws and into Tyler's back.

His grip on me slackened, and he stumbled forward. I landed on my feet and watched Donovan lunge at Brock. The alpha heir screamed and fell to the ground.

Axel focused on Mike as Roxy helped her parents limp away.

Everyone was okay—for now.

"I've let this go on for too long." Tyler spun around, his nostrils flaring. He bent down and pulled a knife from his boot. "I'm going to gut you and let you bleed out slowly."

I'd already hurt him, but he didn't show it. I wished I could reply with a smart-ass comeback, but oh well. Fighting him would have to do.

To prove he didn't scare me, I struck first. I raced toward him, and he frowned.

He hadn't expected that. Everyone feared him.

That was perfect. I jumped, aiming for his throat, and he stepped back. My teeth sank into his shoulder instead, but he grunted in pain before clutching my throat with one hand. He held me away from him, and the immediate lack of oxygen made my brain fuzzy.

I tried pushing my magic, but I couldn't get it to work. He laughed evilly as he raised the hand that held the knife slowly, enjoying the feeling of overpowering me.

Two figures materialized beside me—Murray and Naida coming to my aid. Murray touched Tyler, and the alpha convulsed. When Tyler's grip slackened on my neck, Naida pulled me away and set me down on my feet.

Then everything went into fast motion.

Tyler stumbled out of Murray's grip as the knife fell from his hands. He bent to pick it up, but I rushed over and bit his wrist. He wouldn't hurt anyone else again. Murray punched Tyler in the face over and over again, and Naida touched his arm, filling him with fae magic.

He convulsed, which made his teeth bang together as he dodged Murray's next punch. Tyler kicked Naida in the stomach, and she fell.

"Stop right there!" Mike yelled, pointing a gun at us.

Axel lay on the ground, unconscious. Mike had over-powered him.

No ... things had been going so well.

Donovan tried to reach me, but Brock kicked him in the side, and he landed hard on the ground.

"Never underestimate us." Tyler chuckled and clutched his wrist. "Now my true reign begins. Each of you will be punished, and I'll rule the fae realm as well."

"You know a gun won't stop us," Murray said, glaring at Mike. "We can stop the bullets."

Mike's eyes lit up. "Oh, I know." He motioned to someone behind Tyler.

My eyes landed on Rook right as he shoved the knife into Tyler's back.

Tyler groaned loudly as he fell to his knees. His breathing turned ragged. "How could you?"

"Because you aren't fit to rule," Mike sneered. "I am. You will die knowing I outsmarted you. I'm the strongest, not you." Then, he pulled the trigger.

Tyler opened his mouth, but blood spilled out as he gurgled. His body slumped to the ground, and his breathing stopped.

"What did you do?" Brock screamed, pulling at his hair. "You killed him."

"No." Mike pointed the gun at me. "The fae did with the help of his daughter."

The guy was delusional. We wouldn't let him walk. I charged him, and he fired the gun.

Using my magic, I made the bullet fall to the ground.

When I was within three feet, I lunged at his throat. My teeth sank into Mike's neck, and Brock cried beside me instead of helping his father.

I often found it hard to believe he was a true alpha heir. The guy was a wimp. Before, I'd thought he was strong because he had the arrogant, entitled attitude down pat, but I'd learned so much. Brock was scared shitless. I sympathized with him on that, though. That had been me at one point.

When Mike's blood hit my tongue, something inside me calmed. I didn't want to be like them. Death was too lenient a punishment. Making them live in the face of defeat would be true revenge.

I loosened my hold on him, not wanting to kill him, but Mike grabbed me by the neck.

He lifted me three feet off the ground with one hand. "You pathetic girl. You should've killed me when you had the chance."

Sadie! Donovan cried and ran toward me, but Brock stepped in his way, blocking my mate.

"She didn't choose me, so she dies," Brock said with disgust.

Out of the corner of my eye, I watched Donovan charge Brock. The edges of my vision blurred as Mike cut off my breathing. I tried connecting to my magic, but I couldn't.

I was going to die.

Naida shot magic at him, and he raised the gun to shoot her. He had to be stopped. He was as bad as, if not worse than Tyler. Yes, letting him live would cause him to suffer more, but people would always be at risk if he ever took back control.

I swung my legs toward him, and my claws ripped through his shirt and into his skin.

"Ow!" he yelled in shock and dropped me.

And I did the one thing I'd never wanted to do in my entire life. I lunged for his throat, and before I could think too much about it, I ripped it out. He hit the ground dead.

"You bitch!" Brock screamed and tackled me, wrapping his arms around my waist. Before I could react, Donovan was there. He bit into the alpha heir's legs and dragged him off me.

Terror filtered into me from Brock now that our bond was open. It must have finally clicked that he was outnumbered.

Donovan jumped on Brock and bit his neck, jerking back.

Immense pain filled me for a second before it all vanished as life left his body.

Then an eerie silence wafted around us.

CHAPTER TWENTY-FOUR

Is everyone okay? The guards fighting Egan and the vampires had stopped, and that whole group stood awkwardly in front of one another.

Yes, Axel groaned through the connection as his leg twitched, consciousness coming back to him. He lifted his head, and his gaze went from Tyler to Mike to Brock. *Good, they're all dead.*

I wasn't sure if *good* was the right word.

Roxy was on the back porch with her parents. They weren't bleeding as much now that Tyler was done poking them. They'd finally have a chance to heal.

But first things first. *I'm going to check on the others.*

Naida rushed over to Rook and threw her arms around him. It warmed my heart to see her so happy. I wished I could be part of their reunion, but they deserved privacy, and I had my own people to touch base with.

I charged toward the side of the house as Donovan caught up and ran beside me. I stopped long enough to check Egan and the vampires over.

The enemy wolves averted their gazes, which was odd.

They slunk away, making it clear they didn't plan to attack or fight any longer.

"We're fine," Katherine assured me as she petted my head. "I think the fighting stopped out front too."

It sounded like it had. I couldn't hear any growls, whimpers, or anything, so at least, there was that.

Lillith headed toward the cars. "I'll go grab everyone's clothes. It's hard to communicate when you guys are in wolf form."

The front yard contained more of the same. The enemy wolves were standing down, and Mom rushed over to me in wolf form.

Lillith hurried to the van and pulled out the large bag. We'd brought a few changes of clothes to be safe, which was a godsend. She dropped the bag and unzipped it. "Here, I'll lay them out for you. You can go into the woods behind the house to change." She pulled them out and spread them across the yard so we could find them easily.

In minutes, several wolves had grabbed the clothes and taken off toward the back. Lillith put the bag back in the car. Donovan and I were the last ones to grab our clothes.

"Go on," she said as she slammed the trunk. "I'll bring Egan, Axel, and Roxy theirs."

That was all I needed to hear. I wanted to warn Mom about Rook before she stumbled across him.

We ran through the yard and headed straight into the woods. We shifted back and put on our clothes.

As we stepped from the woods, I heard Mom scream.

She stood five feet from Rook, white as a ghost. He stood between his brother and sister.

"Is it ..." She paused and blinked. "There's no way."

Titan stepped in front of her like Rook posed a threat.

"Hey, Winter." Rook smiled but stayed put. "It's nice to see you again."

"I saw him stab you," Mom whispered. She grabbed Titan's arm and pulled him beside her. She looked at her mate and pointed at the fae. "That's Rook."

"Wait ..." Titan glanced over his shoulder at me. "Sadie's dad?"

Mom glared at Titan. She didn't realize Rook already knew. It would have been comical if it hadn't been so damn heartbreaking.

"That is a shock." Rook frowned and followed Titan's gaze. "I have a daughter who is a young woman now. I missed watching her grow up and wasn't there to protect her." He looked at Murray. "Do the other fae know about her?" His worried tone softened me toward him.

"They do, but Nads realized who she was." Murray nodded at me. "She is under my protection."

"Good." Rook ran a hand through his hair and winced. "I need to recharge. I feel awful."

"First, I need to know something," I said as Donovan and I joined them. "We all thought you were dead. Tyler told Mom he had the blade that could kill you."

"It wasn't." Rook rubbed his hands together. "It packed a punch and knocked me out, but it didn't kill me. I woke up in that room and remained there until you saved me."

"I'm sorry ..." Mom touched his arm. "I had no clue."

"How could you?" he said gently and stuck his hand out to Titan. "I'm Rook, and you are?"

"Titan." The alpha smiled and shook his hand. "I'm glad to see you're okay. It looks like Sadie found both her parents this year."

"You didn't raise her?" Rook's eyebrows rose. "How is that?"

"Tyler had a housekeeper tell me that she'd died, and I made the mistake of believing her." Guilt laced her words. "I took off and stumbled across her by chance just weeks ago."

Egan and Axel strolled out of the woods and made their way to our group.

"It wasn't your fault. Tyler did this." I faced Axel. "Where's Roxy?"

"She went home with her parents to change and help get them settled." Axel pursed his lips. "She wanted some alone time with them, so I figured I should respect that. She said I'll meet them later."

They weren't in the best place to meet anyone right now. They needed time to heal and get over whatever emotional baggage they had.

"We need to go," Murray stated and stepped toward Rook. "The others are probably concerned."

"I know, but I hate to leave Sadie." Rook inhaled sharply, his eyes turning glassy. "I just found out I have a daughter. I want to know so much."

"Rook, I know," Naida said gently. "But we can come visit real soon."

His lavender eyes filled with hope. "Yeah ... if that's okay with you." It was a statement but also a question. He was asking my permission.

"I'd like that." For the first time, maybe I could have a caring mom and dad. It wouldn't be the same as growing up with them, but finding them now was better than never getting the opportunity. "Naida knows where to find me."

"So do I." He winked. "We're connected."

His hand shook as he reached for my arm like he was unsure. When I didn't move out of the way, he touched my arm gently. His hand was cold, which was further proof of the horrible state he was in.

"You should go recharge." I remembered that one day when I'd drained myself completely. "When you're at full strength, I'd love for you to come see me."

"That sounds perfect." He dropped his hand and looked at his brother. "I guess we should go."

"Yes. The guards will be upset when they realize I left them." Murray gestured to Egan. "You better be careful. They're still looking for you."

"Noted." Egan nodded. "You all be safe going back."

"Thank you." They needed to hear it from me even if they were my family. "I hope to see both of you again as well." I wanted Murray and Naida to know it wasn't just Rook I wanted to keep in touch with.

"Hey." Naida hugged me. "We have college to get back to. You'll see me more than you'll like."

"Not possible." I squeezed her back, sad to see her go. We'd missed too much of this semester, so we'd have to start over in the spring if we could smooth it over with the university.

"Let's go." Murray placed a hand on his shoulder. "We need to recharge as well."

Rook frowned. "Goodbye, Sadie. I'll see you soon."

The three of them disappeared.

"That's still unsettling," Torak said as he jogged toward us. "I don't think I'll ever get used to it."

"What was he talking about?" Donovan asked Egan. "Who's looking for you?"

"You know how the fae are." Egan shrugged and glanced around. "They like to be vague and secretive."

"The apple doesn't fall far from the tree," I teased as Blake, and his father stepped into the backyard.

"You did it." Blake's dad looked proud. "Tyler is gone. The pack needs a new alpha."

It sounded like he was insinuating I take on the role. That was something I didn't want. This pack would always hold a special spot in my heart—I'd grown up here—but I did not want to lead them. "And you're the perfect person for that role."

"I don't know." The older man put his hands inside his jeans pockets. "I wasn't the brave one willing to take him down."

"You let us pass when you could have lost the woman most important to you." Those two men were the bravest people I knew. "I say that qualifies." Speaking of which, the overwhelming urge to leave came over me.

Donovan must have felt it too because he took my hand and said, "Look, we need to go back and check on the Hermunslie pack. Do you guys need anything else from us?"

"Uh ... no." Blake shook his head. "I think we're good." He scratched the back of his head. "Sadie, are you sure—"

"Yes." I already knew where he was going. "I'm positive. You and your dad make the most sense." I looked at the others. "Let's check on Roxy and go home."

When Donovan and I walked into our bedroom back at the mansion, my eyes could barely stay open. Between everything that had happened and the Hermunslie pack wanting Donovan and me to become their alpha and alpha mate, it had been a lot to swallow. Donovan had explained to them that it was something he and I needed to talk over. We had discussed it on the way home with Roxy and Axel.

The four of us were a package deal, and it was Axel's family's pack too. All of us agreed that it felt right, unlike Tyler's old pack, and it was something we should do. Axel and Roxy would be the beta and beta mate, and we would run the pack together.

Egan had left us to go check in on his family. I'd wanted to ask him more questions about what Murray had meant, but I didn't have a chance. Part of me wondered if he left before we had time to push more on purpose. But he hadn't seen his family in a long time, and Tyler was no longer a risk, so maybe it was a combination that made him leave so abruptly.

After we took a long shower, I plopped onto the bed, ready to fall asleep. "I could sleep for days. It feels like it's been ages since we've rested."

"You aren't sleeping yet." Donovan crawled on top of me and kissed my lips. *There's something we've gotta do before.* His hand slipped under the shirt I'd just put on, making his intentions very clear.

That small touch warmed my body and took the edge off my sleepiness. *And what's that?* I asked innocently as I deepened our kiss.

He kissed down my face to my neck. When he reached my collarbone, his teeth scratched my skin, and I moaned.

I pushed him off me and onto his back. I wanted him to claim me in the most intimate way possible. My wolf howled inside, and I stood to remove my clothing.

His eyes darkened to almost black as he watched me, and he pulled off his pants and boxers and tossed them aside.

Sit up against the headboard, I commanded. I climbed back onto the bed and straddled him. Our legs rubbed together, and our connection buzzed between us.

His hand slipped between my legs, and he lowered his mouth to my breast. Both his tongue and fingers hit the perfect spots, priming my body for his.

My head fell back as I moved my hips, following his lead. I reached down and touched him, wanting him to feel the same pleasure.

The pressure increased, taking me to the edge. I didn't want it to end, not yet. *Move your hand.*

He obeyed, and I tangled my hand in his hair and pulled his head back so I could kiss him again. I grabbed the hem of his shirt and yanked it off him. Once he was gloriously naked, I ran my hands down his chest, digging my nails into him. He groaned, and I lowered onto him, letting him fill me entirely.

Oh, Sadie, he moaned, and his fingers prodded my hips, pushing me lower onto him.

We moved together, and my lips lowered back to his. I placed my hand on his shoulder, using it as leverage, and bucked hard against him.

The bed creaked as I pounded him into me. His mouth moved to my neck, and I knew this was the moment. This was the last piece to complete our bond.

I need you to know. His teeth grazed the perfect spot. *I love you. The moment I saw you, I knew you were it for me. It scared me so damn much, and I hate that I was ever mean to you. There is no one else for me.* His teeth sank into my skin, and his emotions poured into me like a dam had broken.

He meant every word, and I pushed my emotions into him, allowing them to meld together.

Something snapped into place. I felt his heartbeat inside me and each breath he took. I'd thought we'd been connected before, but it was nothing compared to what I felt for him now.

It was like we were a single being.

A strong orgasm ripped through me like never before, and his body convulsed underneath me as our bond was sealed.

Once we'd stilled, I leaned down and kissed him. From here on out, we were in this together. No one could come between us.

———

THE NEXT MORNING, my pack headed back to the Hermunslie neighborhood. They needed an alpha after all the turmoil they'd gone through with Tyler. Soon, our pack would grow from four to over one hundred.

It was a little overwhelming to think about, but no matter what, the four of us could handle anything together.

For the first time, I felt at peace. A large part of it was due to Donovan and me finally sealing our connection, but it was also more than that. I'd found my family. Not just Rook and Mom but people outside of blood. And the best was yet to come. I could feel it.

As Donovan, Axel, Roxy, and I stepped out of the car and into our new neighborhood, it finally felt like I'd found my home with my mate and my best friend by my side.

The End

ABOUT THE AUTHOR

Jen L. Grey is a *USA Today* Bestselling Author who writes Paranormal Romance, Urban Fantasy, and Fantasy genres.

Jen lives in Tennessee with her husband, two daughters, and two miniature Australian Shepherd. Before she began writing, she was an avid reader and enjoyed being involved in the indie community. Her love for books eventually led her to writing. For more information, please visit her website and sign up for her newsletter.

Check out my future projects and book signing events at my website.
www.jenlgrey.com

ALSO BY JEN L. GREY

The Hidden King Trilogy

Dragon Mate

Dragon Heir

Dragon Queen

The Wolf Born Trilogy

Hidden Mate

Blood Secrets

Awakened Magic

The Marked Wolf Trilogy

Moon Kissed

Chosen Wolf

Broken Curse

Wolf Moon Academy Trilogy

Shadow Mate

Blood Legacy

Rising Fate

The Royal Heir Trilogy

Wolves' Queen

Wolf Unleashed

Wolf's Claim

Bloodshed Academy Trilogy

Year One

Year Two

Year Three

The Half-Breed Prison Duology (Same World As Bloodshed Academy)

Hunted

Cursed

The Artifact Reaper Series

Reaper: The Beginning

Reaper of Earth

Reaper of Wings

Reaper of Flames

Reaper of Water

Stones of Amaria (Shared World)

Kingdom of Storms

Kingdom of Shadows

Kingdom of Ruins

Kingdom of Fire

The Pearson Prophecy

Dawning Ascent

Enlightened Ascent

Reigning Ascent

Stand Alones

Made in the USA
Monee, IL
08 November 2021